Summer Can't Last

Novels telling of the American abroad, his impact on his hosts and how he in turn is changed and influenced by them, are legion, but few if any ring so clear and true as this story, told with skilful understanding and humour and set against the stimulating atmosphere of Edinburgh behind the scenes at Festival time. Ned, a Texan oil man, tries both to fulfil his firm's policy of 'integration' with leading businessmen and politicians, and to surmount the intangible barriers between him and Sarah, the daughter of a building magnate and, first and foremost, an actress. But personal tragedy and other powerful distractions intrude, and the ending of this outstanding novel is unexpected and uncompromising, laying bare all the harshness and poignancy of human emotions.

Summer Can't Last

by

OSWALD WYND

CASSELL · LONDON

CASSELL & COMPANY

35 Red Lion Square · London WC1

and at

MELBOURNE · SYDNEY · TORONTO · CAPE TOWN

JOHANNESBURG · AUCKLAND

———

© *Oswald Wynd 1960*

First published 1960

Set in 11 pt. Garamond type and
printed in Great Britain by
The Camelot Press Ltd., London and Southampton

F·1159

Acknowledgments are made to the Estate of the late Mrs. Frieda Lawrence and to William Heinemann Ltd. for permission to use the quotation from a poem by D. H. Lawrence which appears on page 130.

... There are forces at work which use individuals for purposes far transcending the purpose of keeping these individuals alive and prosperous and respectable and safe and happy in the middle station in life. ...

G. B. Shaw: Preface to *St. Joan*

One

I WENT into that Edinburgh pub with a letter in my pocket from my mother out in Texas asking what kind of girls I had met over here. You could see she was only moderately worried, though, that her real concern was my younger brother Sam, who was due to go off to college in the fall and had already been doing a bit of wing flapping in the nest.

Perhaps my mother had got hold of some illustrated article in *Life* about Americans in Britain, a lot of lean wolves in chromium-decorated cars roaming around ready to stand on the brakes when an Atlantic wind lifted a bit of skirt.

Well, I had the car, and I'm rangy, and I've got the clipped hair-cut, but maybe I lack the simple purpose which drives my countrymen abroad. Mostly I just rode around in my car.

Of course I was in Scotland. Robert Burns seems to have had it pretty easy in his day, but if Scots women were inclined to be careless then, it seems to me a failing they've corrected. They don't dress for men for one thing, they dress to keep out the climate. Most of them wear a kind of uniform, and I've seen some of these uniforms that look like they were woven out of heather. Heather's rough to the touch.

The Melrose wasn't easy to find but I went there because someone told me the fish was good, and up here where nearly everything is boiled or baked you come to look hard for the pleasures of the stomach. The Melrose is just behind Edinburgh's Princes Street and from the outside it looks like the other hundred pubs which are built into the stone walls flanking a lane the sun never gets into. Inside it's a little different. There's an open fire and Victorian mahogany decorating a square central portion given over to bar counters. There is also a smell of fish frying in good fat.

I come from meat country, and the fish habit is something I've only now got the feel for, but when it's fresh it's as good a way of getting your protein as you'll find, even though back home this would sound like lunatic heresy. I had sole, lightly browned in bread-crumbs, out of the North Sea that day, and with it a pint of heavy Scots draught beer. The potatoes were fat French fries which steamed gently when you stuck a fork in them. I was perfectly happy until somebody dropped some gin on my neck.

I don't know why I stood up then, the gin wasn't even iced, but I did. I go up a long way and I stood there about a head over everybody else, an American sticking out of a British crowd and suddenly everyone staring at me. It was a silly situation, I don't know how I looked, I wasn't feeling belligerent or anything, but I was up there and a man in front of me was shouting:

'Damn! That's the rest of my gin gone.'

His glass was empty all right. I must have contacted him on the way up, which wasn't surprising since the Melrose was scarcely offering breathing room at the lunch-hour rush and drinkers were pushed back against the chairs of the eaters.

The man was staring at me. He looked as though his character had been formed by alcohol, his face soft from a steady routine of too many nights with the boys. Under that face was a spotted bow tie and then a waistcoat in a very loud check. He had a high colour which might have been temporary.

'Are you going to buy me another?'

'You think I'm under that obligation?' I asked.

'Mick!'

It was a girl's voice. There weren't many girls in the Melrose but I'd seen a little clump pushed back against some coat-racks. One of them had been working forward and now she caught hold of Mick's arm.

'Don't be a damn' fool!' she said.

It seemed pretty good advice to me but not to Mick.

'You keep out of this, Sarah. This Yank upset my whole glass.'

I don't want to give the impression that the American gets into incidents easily over here, he doesn't. Usually there's a nice little transparent screen pulled down between him and the locals. That screen is more obvious when you're in a pack than when you're solitary, but it's still there to the man alone and in a way you get used to living behind it. It was a little startling to find it snapped up suddenly.

'I think I'd better explain,' I said. 'I got up suddenly because you tipped some of your drink on to my neck. I guess it was a natural reaction. I'm sorry about it.'

Mick wasn't accepting any responsibility for a wobbly glass and he used a couple of routine swear words which didn't mean anything in themselves but which were none the less venom-ous in the way they were directed at me. I felt warm under my shirt and knew that this warmth, bright red, was coming up into my neck.

'Angus,' the girl said, jerking her head to one side. 'Angus, for heaven's sake stop this!'

Angus turned. He had been part of the background in the crowd, a head of greying hair obviously under the care of a tonsorial artist and now he showed a face created by a masseur, flesh contoured to bone by a lot of pounding. I was certain that Angus had been perfectly conscious of the little row boiling up behind him but avoided getting involved for as long as possible.

'Mick being bloody-minded again?'

It was a voice I couldn't place. In Britain you hear the local voice; the local voice with overtones of a superior education or superior politeness; and B.B.C. English. Angus spoke with a

3

tang of Scots, but it seemed as carefully added as the drops of bitters in a Martini. He might be a Scot apologizing for years at Oxford.

'I just want another gin, that's all,' Mick said. 'It's the least he could do, isn't it? It's what I'd do if I knocked someone's bloody gin out of his hand.'

Angus spoke quietly.

'It's only a couple of nights, Mick, since you sat on my drink. You didn't get me another. I didn't complain.'

The girl laughed and one or two of the males beyond Angus, but none of the businessmen with the lifted, serious faces; they just went on chewing against the clock. They had been half-waiting for something to happen in the Melrose, but without any real hope. When those heads bent again over food I knew the crisis was over.

Angus put an arm over Mick's shoulders, swinging him round. Then Angus smiled at me pleasantly, closing the episode, even over Mick's mutterings.

I went back to my fish. It had settled a little on a chilled plate and the parsley garnish drooped under the weight of solidifying grease. The beer, which they never ice, was now tepid. I knew there were people waiting for my seat and got out of it as soon as I could, making my way to the back of the pub where I'd left my coat.

There wasn't room to put the coat on, I just hugged it to me and began to push towards the swinging doors to the street. And then I had one of those impulses which are probably the direct result of a steady attendance at Sunday school in youth, and which can be disastrous to Americans abroad. I stopped pushing and turned towards the bar again. Right behind Angus I said:

'Look . . . I'd like to buy a round.'

It's not easy to create a silence in a pub at the rush hour but about eight people stopped talking and looked at me. I had the feeling that was all they were going to do, that no one was going to say a single word. Then the girl spoke up.

'That's rather sweet,' she said.

4

It is probably precisely what it was. I was threatened by the heat flush again and my hands were a bit clammy.

'It's amiable of you,' Angus told me. 'But really, you mustn't feel . . .'

'I want to!'

I didn't now, but there I was, getting in towards the bar counter. They may have seen I was running a temperature and in charity applied good manners to help me cool down. I had to face five men and three girls in turn, asking each what they would like, and my overcoat kept getting in the way as I handed out drinks with one hand.

'Well, cheers,' Angus said.

The others said it, too, lifting glasses towards me, even Mick, bow-tie slightly askew, smiling a little as though he had somehow contrived this.

'You're a colonel in the Air Force,' Angus said.

It was an announcement. He expected to be right.

'No. Civilian. I'm a technician helping to build an extension to your oil refinery at Grangemouth.'

'A civilian!'

It was one of the girls. She was staring at me as though I had to be completely re-assessed. Angus looked, too, apparently made uneasy by an encounter with an American, out of the tourist season, who didn't fit into the usual classifications.

One of our national weaknesses is to tell too much about ourselves too soon, and I began to answer questions they hadn't asked. Once started it wasn't easy to stop. I found myself talking about American capital investment in Scotland, little beads of sweat coming out on my forehead as I did it.

They sipped and watched me. In ten minutes they knew more about me than I'd find out about them in months of acquaintance, and I was feeling a little sick. Still I went on with it, sounding like a business efficiency expert after the third highball in the club car of a transcontinental streamliner. I was drinking whisky, a small glass in my great ham of a hand.

Even at college I never thought of myself as potential gogetter material at all. I did a B.A. in Literature, meaning to travel on to an M.A. and teaching, but my terrified family cut in here. They couldn't stand the prospect of their eldest living out his life as a poverty-stricken egghead, and I listened to them and went to technical school, turning from Shakespeare to refining oil.

I don't think the switch-over set up any chain of mental disturbance in me, at least not that I'm conscious of, but perhaps it does make me, in the company of declared intellectuals, just a little inclined to place myself as the practical man with his large feet in British hand-made shoes set very firmly on concrete.

And I was doing just that with these declared intellectuals, for that's what they were all right; all eight of them sent out corporate and personal proclamations to this effect. In that crowded pub they were clearly isolated from the rest of humanity by whatever form of creative activity obsessed them.

The women are normally the first thing I look at in any room, but for some reason I hadn't with these three, even at the girl who had come to my assistance. Now, needing someone to help me quit carrying on like a London West End actor impersonating an American, I looked at her again. And looking at her I was able to slow down. I was even able to come to a stop and take a deep breath.

She was a pretty girl. I knew her name was Sarah. It's a nice name, nicely balanced, with no pretensions, ideal for a woman so well endowed she can do without artificial trimmings. This girl was so endowed. She was wearing a chain store adaptation of a Paris model, a suit that only women could possibly appreciate. To me it was hideous, belted across the bottom, and it was a kind of miracle that in the thing she still managed to appear desirable.

Sarah wore more make-up than is customary in her country. Up here the girls mostly treat aids to beauty as something still in the experimental stage to be used with extreme caution. But Sarah's lipstick was a deep, thick red. After it you noticed her hair, black, sleek, far longer than the fashion, almost to her shoulders. Even with one of those cocker-spaniel backside cuts you'd have still wanted to go on looking at her, but I was at once grateful that she hadn't let anyone monkey with her hair, just brushing it and letting it fall like that.

Only one of the other women there that day comes into this. She was in a black suit, rigidly tailored, and about her was the suggestion of youth stretched to the breaking point, of a continuous, laborious attempt to be something she wasn't any more. You had the feeling that very soon she was just going to have to give up and wait to play mums. In Hollywood, if she'd been box office, they could still have done quite a lot with adhesive tape.

It wasn't a smart guess that she was an actress, but it gave me a clue to the rest of them, to Sarah, too. And then I spotted in Sarah that slight posing which people in her trade never get away from; even a sudden movement is something with stage directions tacked on to it. A couple of the men were like that, too, not Angus or Mick, but two tall ones in their thirties, in old but tightly smooth suitings of a style that the American male very wisely won't take to, probably because our bodies have too many knobs and angles.

The sudden silence was almost as bad as my talk had been. I was back against the bar with my overcoat bulging out in front of me as my only defence against strangers towards whom I had projected my personality. The actress in black obviously liked Americans to stick to type and she prodded me, smiling.

'I've heard that Grangemouth has become a little America.'

'We haven't managed to alter the cooking much, ma'am.'

She didn't like that *ma'am*. It made her next words prickle.

'Odd, you know. One never meets anyone who's ever been to Grangemouth. All I've seen of it is a lot of huge pipes on the skyline.'

'That's us all right. Quite a nice little place when you come down into it and it isn't raining or there isn't a fog from the river.'

'Do you have a house there?'

7

'No, I have lodgings. I have a landlady who makes me eat high tea. It isn't home baking, either.'

Sarah smiled at me.

'I know,' she said. 'Iced cakes and three kinds of scones.'

'Plus a peculiar kind of fish I get most Tuesdays. It's preserved, painted a dirty brown on the outside. It looks like it might have come out of an Egyptian tomb.'

Being in a minority of one or two with a crowd of British of this variety produces in the American a kind of chemical antipathy. It isn't just that we're on the defensive, it's that we sense defeat from the outset, that we are under control, and a type of chain reaction has been started which is what they want.

Now it was the girl. She'd sprung the trap when I thought she was helping. I had been led neatly into that inevitable tone of critical irritation with the physical circumstances of my life in a strange country. And the horrible thing is that I put on this act because the British want it; it's something they expect from us, and I don't feel it personally in the least. For instance, I quite like that painted fish.

But here I was again, on the British way of life, to a polite audience who were getting precisely what they expected and thinking how perfectly bloody these new Romans are.

I could say quite a lot about this business of being the new Greeks. For that is, of course, how the British see themselves; in decline, yes, but in a sunset that has its own fading radiance. Already a kind of literary nostalgia permeates the scene, and there is a sort of intense, inverted pleasure in the relics of the old order, in the Guardees who dress exactly like Daddy did even though Daddy's kind of war isn't available any more. You carry your furled umbrella towards the future and are prepared to go down into the barbarian dark sipping a gin with just the right amount of pink added.

This, of course, is no balanced picture, it's just the occasional reaction of an American who gets mad easily. It was my reaction that day to the situation into which I had flat-footedly walked. And I think I was madder than usual because it is not the sort of thing that you expect to have happen to you in a

8

Scots pub. I felt this little scene ought to be being played out four hundred miles to the south. Down there one was more or less geared for it and I'd always seemed to have an escape route open, the night train to Scotland. This was almost my own ground; I'd learned how to feel my way around in it.

Or so I thought. Maybe that was just illusion, too, that I'd been creating a fiction when I thought I'd caught something of this place. I'd thought there was a kind of basic rowdiness in the Scot which made him approachable on simple human terms, which, of course, means my terms. I'd liked their sentimental materialism which is the kind of thing we're comfortable with back home.

But these were Greeks all right, a whole little clump of them. And they weren't English, either, weren't importations, for all that an experience of England was a part of what they were offering.

The girl who was fighting the years behind her was the only one who was really bent now on hounding me down. Her name was Edna. She had disliked me at first only on principle, but now added to that the bitterness of the professional entertainer who has been looked at by a male with no lights coming on.

'I've always wondered about these American communities. We forget that they're everywhere, all over the world. And you have to live isolated, to maintain that standard of living of yours. Do you have P.X.s at Grangemouth?'

'No, ma'am.'

She smiled.

'I don't expect that matters. You'll have other arrangements.'

'Yes. We have the captains of the tankers. They bring us corn on the cob in deep freeze and those really big California ripe olives.'

'I know,' said Edna, through the teeth of another smile. 'Quite tasteless!'

'It's the getting two bites out of an olive that matters to us, ma'am.'

I'll say this for my performance, they were a little bit on

9

edge now themselves, as far as I could see, all of them, including Angus. Sarah was looking at me, standing quite still, just looking at me.

'We have typical U.S. evenings,' I told them. 'You know, we eat a lot. Then we watch home movies, then we dance a little. We have real highballs. We get the Bourbon off the tankers, too. Now there's no need for any of you ever to go to Grangemouth. I'll be on my way. So long.'

It wasn't surprising that they didn't any of them try to stop me. I got clear and pushed my way past the crowds at the central bar, past the tables where a new instalment of businessmen were chewing seriously just above their newspapers. The Melrose had double swinging doors and I pushed at both of them, suddenly being clutched at by the damp Scots winter cold.

I put on my coat and then I guess I must have gone fast up the narrow pavement. If I had been liable to indigestion I'd have been reaching in my pockets for tablets, but it happens I'm not.

'Hey!'

I didn't look round the first time.

'Hey!'

It was Sarah. She was running. The new suits aren't designed for that, only for walking downstairs or sitting on bar stools. It was merely humane to wait for her to come up. I wasn't even curious in those seconds.

'I want a lift in your Cadillac,' she said.

'It's a Pontiac. Have you eaten?'

'No. I don't want to.'

'I didn't mean to create that big a disturbance.'

'Oh, don't be so damn' full of yourself! I just happen to want to get away from them, that's all.'

'Via me? The Texan stranger?'

She looked at me, her eyes very dark.

'Are you frightened?' she asked.

We went to the parking place. I have a noisy looking car with a quiet engine and when we were inside it all you could hear was the flip of the wipers trying to deal with the congealing damp. It wasn't raining, it was just the usual cloud condensing with a lot of soot from chimneys. I pushed around in the traffic, getting down on to Princes Street.

'You'll have to tell me where to go. I only know how to get in and out of this town.'

'I want out of it,' Sarah said. 'That is, if this is your afternoon off.'

'It's my day off.'

'Where would an American take a girl out of Edinburgh?'

'The Forth Bridge.'

She laughed then. It was the first time I'd heard her laugh.

'Fine,' she said.

Sarah smoked her own cigarettes. I knew she would do that, mine came from a tanker captain. I got through the suburbs and the limited zone and then let the car move. The road is a switchback, with poor visibility, but good cornering, and we ran smoothly under dripping trees.

'I thought for a moment,' Sarah said, 'that you were going to hit Mick.'

'Well, I wasn't ever going to.'

'Does your company have rules about how you conduct yourselves with the natives?'

'Look . . . if you came in this car just to rub my nose in what happened back there . . .'

'I didn't!'

'All right. Maybe if we're lucky when we get to the Forth Bridge there'll be a train going over.'

She sat very quietly in her corner of that broad front seat and we must have gone five miles like that, until I said:

'Like the radio? It's a big set, specially installed. You can pick up the American Forces Network in Germany. I listen a lot when I'm driving. I find it's a change from the sound of rain on the roof.'

'Did you bring your dislike of us over with you?' Sarah asked. 'Or has it developed over here?'

'You've got it wrong. I don't have those feelings. They're

not a permanent part of me. They just happen sometimes. And it's always me. I mean, it comes from not sitting quietly in my corner and eating my soup. And I always have plenty of warning, too, so that I'm not making excuses for myself. And don't get this wrong, I'm having a great time over here. I'm enjoying myself, and I don't just mean with the olive-eaters, either. I know a lot of fellows at the refinery and I've gone home with them and met their wives and we've had evenings at the pub. And sometimes we get in a car and go off for picnics into the Highlands on a good Saturday. I won't even be sour about the weather . . . there have been some pretty beautiful days.'

Sarah looked at the road. She was sitting with her hands folded on her knees, almost as though she was holding her skirt there. Between two of her very thin, long fingers, was the cigarette smoking away. The seat was a comfortable one, but she wasn't using the comfort of it.

'You never told us your name,' she said.

It seemed almost impossible that when I'd given them so much I'd missed that.

'Ned. Don't say you like it. It sounds like the old horse in a kid's story.'

'I don't like it,' Sarah said.

And that was exactly all there was between us when we got out at South Queensferry and stood looking at the Forth Bridge which you couldn't see the other end of because of the fog. A tired looking corvette painted grey was creeping under the central span, and you could see the ruins of fortifications to guard the bridge which would never be used again. The car ferry pulled out and we watched it go. I nearly said that in any other country they would have built a road bridge alongside the railway one thirty years ago, but I didn't.

I had no idea of where I was going with this girl, or if I was going anywhere. There was a flat, dead calm between us, with no more colour in it than there was colour in that water out there which moved with an oily grey persistence towards the sea. Sarah stood with her head lifted as though there was something important up on the bridge if she could only find it. It was cold, but her face didn't take on a pinched in, shrivelled look as she waited. Sarah didn't wear any heather mixture but she was a child of this cold, too, and her blood was in the right solution to take it. She looked at me suddenly, smiling, and she had small, very good, just slightly pointed teeth.

'It's unsettling for a man, isn't it? Not knowing whether a new girl is an easy make or not? Well, I'm not, Ned.'

Two

We went for a drink much later on, when they opened, not to a pub but to a place by the river which had been done up as tourist bait with plenty of whitewash and wrought-iron and mugs hanging along beams. But with the law the way it is we had to drive around a lot before that could happen and Sarah got an absolutely solid build-up on me. She knew that I came from Abilene where the country starts to swell up into the great mountains and that my dad was in the wholesale drug business which he'd got into after being a farmer and that I had a brother called Sam and a sister called Louise and that my mum was a Daughter of the Star of Texas. She knew that I was a Baptist and a Democrat like Truman and that I liked dogs but cats gave me a funny tingling along my spine. She knew what time I got up in the morning and what records I bought and that I made the first basketball team in High School but only got on to the second at college and that only in my Junior year. She knew that I meant to stay in the oil business until I was fifty-eight and then quit before I got a heart attack. And that I wanted four kids exactly because every American family has got to double itself if we're going to keep up with the Russians.

I knew that Sarah was an actress, but then I'd known that in the Melrose.

She sat well on a stool. She had a thin, long neck, not

scrawny, flesh where there ought to be, and though I don't like to say this, there was something birdlike about the sudden movement of her head. She almost jerked her head at me when I had said something that interested her, but that wasn't too often.

I noticed that Sarah always knew what to do with her hands, and that they were in use a great deal, a bit of exhibitionism here, maybe, the knowledge that those long, thin fingers could do a lot of talking on their own. I found myself watching when she reached out for a glass and curled her fingers around the stem. On the smallest she was wearing a large ring with a flashy paste ruby.

She wasn't as good-looking as I'd thought back in the Melrose. Sarah hadn't that quality of looks which automatically decorates and sometimes, when I was talking, and her interest in me, slight enough yet, wasn't stirred at all, her face stayed quite dead. She wasn't listening and she didn't make any social effort of pretence, as though she were out of the habit of paying men this compliment, if she'd ever had the habit. She sat by me, a neutral, surrounded by a kind of calm vacuum.

With Sarah's second drink there was a change. I hung on to my first, not being a drinking man when I have a car to drive, and my slowness here gave me my first real advantage. Suddenly we were moving at different speeds and I was able to do the watching, seeing her boosted by that Martini and guessing that this was pretty much a habit. I didn't ask about the third, I just ordered it. But that one didn't go so quickly.

'You must have thought it odd, Ned. Have you been picked up in Scotland before?'

'No. I'm told I don't go to the right places.'

She laughed.

'I wanted to escape from that pub. I'd have run after anyone.'

'Thanks.'

'Ned! I'm beginning to think I could take quite a lot of you.

15

There's a kind of wonderful innocence in all that life history. You've had a dull life, haven't you?'

I looked at her for quite a long time, right into her eyes. Then I said:

'Yes.'

'I haven't. Sometimes I wish to hell I'd followed all the indicators. Everything was marked out plainly enough. What did you think of them today . . . my friends in the Melrose?'

'I've never seen anything like them up here.'

'They'd be flattered. They don't think there *is* anything like them up here. They're what I ran away from to go to London. And today I came back . . . for the first time in three years. I was being received into the family again when you did your little act. They were being very nice about having me back. We'd even reached the point where Angus had offered me a part in his new production on radio. With Edna in the lead, of course. You didn't like Edna?'

'No.'

'No one does, poor soul. But she's our queen for all that. She may be fading but she has a lovely voice, did you notice? When you hear her on the radio she can make you weep. Oh, you needn't look like that, she can. You know the stops are being pulled out but you still react. Sometimes even in London I used to tune in to Edna's suffering Scots female. There was something stabilizing about hearing Edna's voice from four hundred miles away. The little queen, who's been doing that for twenty years. And never silly enough to risk leaving the little kingdom.'

'You left; what happened?'

Sarah stared at her glass. She swilled the liquor around in it.

'Oh, I went to Birmingham. To the Rep. I was supposed to have been a success. I stayed for twenty months and as far as I know no one wrote in to say they were tired of seeing my face all the time. You wonder why people who go to Rep often don't do that. It's supposed to be a wonderful training. Actually you find yourself being you whether it's *Hedda*

Gabler or *Rookery Nook*. On the whole I preferred farce. I've got a wonderful scream.'

'Twenty months. After that?'

Sarah smiled.

'London. My big chance. West End. Good-bye to Rep. The play lasted a week. I had two walk-ons in television and a part in a B picture . . . a very small part. Aren't I being honest? Why are you looking me over like that?'

'I was just thinking you give the impression of being pretty expensive.'

'Damn you! My daddy is prosperous. I told you all the indicators were there. There was no need for me to bother about doing something with myself. The sensible thing to do would have been to stay at home and not learn about failure. I could have had a nice double flat in Edinburgh's New Town, and a cupboard full of the sort of clothes you chuck out at the end of the season because they bore you a little, and a sports car at the door. All that and a month on the Riviera at Xmas. The man was waiting. He still seems to be, the poor fool.'

'You're not thinking about it again?'

Sarah shook her head.

'No, my conditioning was all wrong. You see, I came on the scene a little too early. Dad was doing quite well but he hadn't become a director. So I wasn't sent to quite the right school, just one of those Edinburgh ones where you come home at night. Now my younger sister . . . she's getting the proper treatment. There is a boarding school in Fife which has the biggest concentration of Bentleys on speech day north of St. Albans. She's there. She plays a splendid game of hockey, and I'm quite certain never mentions me to her pals.'

'Did you come home because you were beat?'

'My dear, I don't think three drinks entitle you to the answer to that one.'

'Have another?'

'Very well. At your risk. I might really begin to talk.'

But the next drink shut her up completely. It was a little

strange. She didn't say another word while she finished it. Then she looked at me and slowly began to push herself off the stool.

'Let's get out of here,' she said.

Outside I began to remember that Sarah hadn't eaten anything in the middle of the day or since. When we were in the car I asked her where she would like to eat. She shook her head.

'Nowhere. I'm taking you home. It's what you all want . . . to see the inside of a lovely Scots home. Well . . . get this thing moving. Up to the heights. Know the way to Morningside?'

'No.'

'I'll show you. I'll drive if you like.'

'I think not. Look . . . ought you to go home like this? I mean, wouldn't it be better to eat something first?'

'My ma is lying smitten in her bed. I have to be there at meal-times. That's why I came home, son. I wasn't beat. I just had to answer a cry of need from my family. Poor old Mum.'

I didn't much like her tone right then. It may be small town of me, but there are some ways you don't talk about your mother, whether you've had a few drinks or not. As I drove I was conscious of Sarah looking at me. It was dark now, but there were lights on the road and lights from the dash. We were cut off by dark and those lights, the two of us. Sarah began to laugh, quietly, almost contentedly, at some private joke which would be a little spoiled by any attempt to share.

She could keep her jokes. I was deciding right then that I'd see her home and go through with anything she wanted about meeting her family and after it say good night at the door and that would be that.

'Ned! Stop looking so sulky. You had it coming to you.'

'Meaning what?'

'Sweetie, you gave me you for hours. I had the whole of you that's for public exhibition, even what you felt about basketball. I needed those drinks.'

'Okay, I talk too much.'

'Yes, about the wrong things. Want me to light you a cigarette?'

'I don't like your kind.'

She laughed again. She folded her arms and seemed to hug herself, laughing.

'Ned, dear, stop the car.'

'Why . . . ?' I began.

Then I stopped the car.

Sarah just moved over from her side of the wide seat. She put both arms over my shoulders and let them hang down the back, quite limp. She kissed me and her breath smelt of gin. Then I wasn't noticing things like that. Somehow everything just stopped when she wanted it, and she was back in her corner again.

'Funny,' she said. 'I've been wanting to do that all afternoon. I think it's your nose. It's cute.'

She had her compact out and was using it in the dim light, peering a little.

'Hadn't we better get going?' she asked. 'I've just remembered that it's fried fish tonight. Is that what you had for lunch in the Melrose?'

'Yes.'

'Ned, dear, don't sit there with your hands on the wheel as though you'd just undergone a tremendous emotional experience. Start the engine!'

I started the engine and we moved off.

'Are you sure you won't mind fried fish again?'

'Of course I won't mind it!'

'I'm glad your digestion is all right. But then I should have known, you'd have told me this afternoon if it hadn't been.'

I don't think I'd been so mad for years. I drove the car like that, too, carefully, but very fast. And I didn't get much satisfaction out of that. I knew Sarah was enjoying it.

I'd never been in Morningside. At night it didn't look very exotic, it was lit by blue lights, and, where these weren't, by gas still, and there was a lot of dark stone, and hedges and the smell of buses and damp. Tyres hissed on the asphalt. I had to brake once for a dog. It walked across like it was on a pedestrian crossing, though it wasn't, waggling its behind. Most British dogs look like they knew ninety per cent of the people they meet up with are their slaves. A lot of dogs take advantage of their happy world and are extremely bad-tempered. This one was sniggering at us, I'm sure of that. I thought of people in the war going without their sausages to keep dogs happy. A woman in a train once told me she gave most of her meat ration to a cocker spaniel, and she said that as though it proved she was a human being.

'Right here,' Sarah said. 'We live up a drive. And you'll have to take a big sweep to get this thing through the gates. They're on the narrow side.'

The tyres crunched on gravel. I could smell wet grass and wet evergreens and then the headlights picked out a huge black Daimler sitting in front of a huge black house. In some way that house and that car looked like relations. There was a sort of porch with stone pillars, but, whatever they might say, the feel was Roman, not Greek, that sense of weight. Here was the kind of house you couldn't alter outside from one generation to the next without blasting. It would be the people in it who changed.

I didn't see a light in the hall until we were out of the car and then it glimmered through a curved fanlight, not more than fifteen candlepower. The Scots are the greatest turners off of switches you'll find anywhere. They rarely have a light burning where they aren't, even if they're coming back soon, and none of the shops downtown dream of leaving their windows illumined. What's the use of showing your wares when the doors aren't open? It's like Sunday all week at night and on Sunday after dark you wonder if there hasn't been an atomic fall-out.

Sarah was at the door, making scraping noises at an invisible keyhole.

'I've got a flashlight in the car.'

'Don't be silly, I'll find it in a minute.'

She found it. The door opened into a hall which was illumined with the tone of reds and green you see in one of those Arab cafés in Paris. The glow came from an enormous central lantern in wrought-iron. It was a kind of pilot light these people left on, probably because they were rich. Anyway, Sarah found a switch and suddenly there was a glowing against panelling.

I could see the furnishings now. There was money here all right, a Turkey carpet with a ruby lustre, Chinese deadwood chairs with serpents for legs, enormous pots of blue and pink which could never have had a decent use in old Cathay, but might, I suppose, have been manufactured for the export trade in the days when people used palms. The ceiling was very high and a great stair went curving away at the bottom of the hall with what I took to be a stained-glass window on the half-landing, though now it was just mud-coloured.

It was cold in there, colder than outside. And to the cold was added a feeling of damp passages beyond doors, places that even in summer never got dried out. And because it was a hall no one ever thought about heat; they would have as soon thought about trying to heat the area just beyond the platforms in a railway terminus. The hall was for transit, not for loitering. No one had ever sat in those deadwood chairs, even to use the telephone.

'This way,' Sarah said, and opened a door on the left.

Switches clicked again. I saw a very large room indeed, padded and neutral, with thick carpets and heavy, overstuffed furniture, the overall colour scheme a kind of beige. The hall, for all its solemnity, had struck a personal note, it was some-one's idea of what a hall should look like if you'd made the grade. But in this room there wasn't a hint of the individual behind all the equipment; it was as though the owner, looking at those dimensions, had given up and sent for the professional decorator in the town's most expensive department store. The result was like the lounge in one of those hotels where the dinner menu would always start off with brown Windsor soup.

I couldn't see any books or magazines, though there was a fire burning and people must use the place. Even the big cabinet television set had its doors firmly closed.

'I must go and see Mother,' Sarah said. 'I'll tell Father you're here. Oh . . . the drinks are on that table. Help yourself.'

Sarah spoke quietly. Her voice seemed flattened, oddly polite, as though the room demanded politeness. You couldn't imagine a row in that place, with people shouting. The heavy drapes would have absorbed most of the noise anyway and made it all seem rather futile. She smiled at me; it was almost a polite smile, small and controlled, as though once again, and sharply, this room reminded Sarah that under this roof she was living on the kind of sufference parents do impose on their older children. This wasn't the world of home Sarah remembered and the place had a neutral power to impose its will on her.

I thought I knew exactly what Sarah felt here. Back in Abilene my people don't live any more in the house we had when I was a kid. They've built themselves a kind of middle-aged success symbol, for which they paid architect's fees alone of about three thousand dollars. It has a flat roof, and masses of glass and a patio and a pool beyond it. Some of the furniture I still recognize but mostly my feeling in those rooms is very far from being back with the old folks at home. There's nothing static about my people, they're still pushing away at their own lives, getting places. I guess the rocker-on-the-porch age had vanished for ever, at least in my part of the country. But it must have been restful in a way, giving you a feeling of escape still open, a sense of permanence in what you'd left behind subject only to man's natural mortality.

Sarah wouldn't have been brought up in this hotel lounge. When she was a kid there hadn't been a drive to the front door, and almost certainly no Daimler.

I poured a gin carefully and took it over to the fire. The decorators had pulled out the original Victorian mahogany with vast overmantel, which must certainly have once been there, and installed in its place a thing of tiles, brown and so shiny that they made even a fairly healthy fire look somehow sad.

I sat down in the sort of chair that was too well built ever to get hollows from use, and was caught suddenly in one of those moments of near panic that can happen in a room that's always going to be so much more static than the people who use it. You get it when you're in a town for a bit when you don't know anyone, doing a job, but with the evenings absolutely empty. There's bed waiting after a meal or the pictures or the place where they let you look at television if you don't want to do it in your nice comfortable bedroom. And everyone about you is moving towards that time when they pay their bill and check out. It's unhealthy to allow your mind to dwell on your own rootlessness, but sometimes it's forced on you, especially when you look at the older ones, the expensive hairdos bent slightly over glossy magazines. Sometimes there's just the sound of faint music somewhere, coming from other people's lives.

I knew what all this meant for me. I'm not the type that can really make effective use of walking free. I ought to have a vast load of commitments, even my sexual urges are a by-product of a basic need to be a daddy, with a lot of noise waiting for me, and a huge mortgage and a car that will be paid for a year after we get our new one. I couldn't go hunting for a woman as an end in itself to save me. My lusts are tied up with aprons and something bubbling on a cooker. A lot more men have the papa urge than psychiatrists allow for. It may be why I always notice houses and the shape of rooms and the feel of them and why I hate modern furniture so much.

I stretched out my legs and looked at my feet. I hadn't got any suits over here, but I do like their shoes. These ones were hand-made for me on a last by a bootmaker in Edinburgh. You go there and they make models of your feet in wood and ever afterwards, wherever you may be, you can order your shoes from them, unless you get terrible bunions. Even then I believe that if you send them the dimensions of your abnormalities they'd still be able to fit you. I'd spent about three hundred dollars on shoes in that place and I knew I was never going to regret it. Every night I took off my shoes and fitted them in special holders.

The door opened and Sarah came in. She stopped, looking at me. I must have seemed pretty relaxed with my legs stretched out like that, and it startled her. She was almost as surprised as if she'd come in and found me with my feet right up on that brocaded sofa. My posture didn't offer the respect this room demanded in tribute, and I must have suggested the kind of casual insolence towards place which the British don't like in Americans.

'You got your drink?' she said, just a shade stiffly.

I stood.

'Yes. Can I mix you one?'

'Well . . . all right.'

There was complete silence while I got another gin. I made it weaker, as though instinct told me the kind of drink Sarah would take in that house. She sipped, doubtfully for a moment, and then suddenly looked up with a smile.

'Ned, I'm sorry. Daddy can't join us tonight. He's working on some report in his study. He said he might have coffee with us later. But he's having a tray in there.'

'There's no need to apologize.'

'Well . . . I brought you back to meet the family.'

You wouldn't have thought the girl I'd met in the Melrose could be as nervous as this. I knew now that it was those gins which had made her issue the invitation and the effect of them had worn off.

'Mummy wants to see you though.'

Mummy? It was 'Ma' outside, and maybe a lot of other things. But this house was a bully, even the stranger could feel that.

'I think I should explain, Ned. She's in bed, you see. And she probably always will be, so the doctors say. She had a heart attack.'

I felt that little jolt of fear which must be not unlike the reaction in the Middle Ages to talk of the plague. Heart

24

trouble is something pretty near all of us, something sent by the Fates even though Fate is the kind of way we eat and live.

Sarah lit a cigarette.

'We can't tell her, of course. I mean that she'll never be active again. The doctor says we're not to. Mother's a golfer, you see. It was a kind of religion. Sometimes she played eighteen holes twice a day, which I suppose is madness at fifty-two.'

'Is she a bridge player, too?'

Sarah looked at me sharply.

'Yes. I see you know that pattern. She's a bridge player, too. Only that has to stop as well. She can't have any excitement. She lies up there and . . . oh, well. . . .'

Sarah put down her drink on the polished beige tiles that served as a mantelshelf. She looked at the fire and spoke carefully.

'The doctor's idea is that mother's bedroom should be a kind of centre of the house. He wants to give her that interest. So we all go up there. I mean, it's a sort of sitting-room now. Most visitors are taken up. I never use this place. I . . .'

Sarah broke off and then added, as though she had been meaning to say something else:

'Mother has her own TV. Would you like to go up now, Ned?'

'Why, sure.'

We went up those long curving stairs and our feet didn't make a sound on the thick carpeting. Our movement was so still that I could hear my breathing and I thought Sarah's. There was no smell of medicines on that upper landing, just the heavy tang of chrysanthemums. All the doors were shut except one, and light came out of that and noise, music from a television programme.

The bed was placed so that it commanded a view of the door and it was the first thing you saw, a high-backed bed, in white enamel and gilt with a long, silk-covered stool in the same finish at the foot of it. It was an extra-wide double, covered in some kind of damask, and right in the middle of it was a big woman. It was a big bed but she gave the impression of using all of it, propped up against pillows, in some kind of blue *négligé* thing which trailed bits on the gold damask. At each side of the bed huge, white-silked, fringed lamps sent out a filtered, almost gentle light, like something from an oil lamp. It was a luxurious room, with a neutral luxury, and it was a completely absurd room for the woman using it. You could see at once how she had just moved in here after the decorator had gone and filled the cupboards with her tweed skirts and golf woollies, with some solid plain things for bridge and drinks with the girls, and behind that again a few specimens of the kind of clothes a director's wife has to wear sometimes, but which she hated putting on.

I saw first her golf wrists, a man's wrists, and big, strong-fingered hands which weren't made any more feminine by diamonds glittering. Her name was Ella, and after a time I don't think she would have minded if I'd called her that.

'Turn off that set, Sarah! These programmes. I never watched television so much before. It puts me off eating. That's probably a good thing.'

When she laughed I knew how uneasy she was. It had been a deep powerful laugh, but now she was afraid to let herself go. Anything might be just a little bit too much. She'd had a full life, packing it with the two things she wanted, and now she didn't have either of them. It made her catch her breath sometimes and lie there when there wasn't a noise in the room listening to her heart, and wondering if that was the right kind of thumping or whether she ought to call the doctor again. The phone was there by her hand, a special phone in white enamel.

Ella Baillie, a big woman who looked natural in bars and at home in them drinking whisky. She had a large head and on it hair cut short and carefully waved. Her hairdresser must be coming regularly still. They would keep up with everything like that which was possible. Her friends would come, too, when they might be playing bridge, and they'd all look a bit like her and a bit uneasy at being in a sick room because that was the kind of thing they'd managed, most of them, to avoid one way or another.

Some people would have learned a lot lying in bed with heart trouble but not Ella Baillie, because she wasn't looking. All she would allow herself to see was the life she had known and was going to know again soon. She asked me if I played golf and I said I knocked a ball around but was no good and she told me now that I was in Scotland where there was a golf course every five miles I ought to settle to it. If I'd come before she was put in her bed she'd have told me that I could go on playing golf as long as I could stand.

Sarah said absolutely nothing at all. We both sat down, a little awkwardly, flanking that television set which had been brought forward on a wheeled table so that it was near the bed. The big box was between Sarah and me and it kept me from seeing her expression as she looked at her mother. Sarah must have been looking at Ella Baillie because the way things were in that room you just had to look at the bed.

Ella's voice had been toned down a little by illness, but it was still loud. It went with that heavy-featured face and her big, dark eyes. There was the only resemblance to Sarah I could see at all, in those eyes. For the rest mother and daughter might have been strangers.

She didn't talk like her daughter, either. Her accent was Scots thinned a little by having money, but not by any means watered down to the kind of shrill politeness of tortured vowels I sometimes heard on Princes Street. I could just hear Ella Baillie, not getting out of a bunker, letting the world know what she thought about that.

'Have you given your friend a drink?'

'Yes, Mother.'

'Well, I should hope so. But I'm never quite sure what's going on downstairs these days. Was there a fire on in the drawing-room?'

'Yes, Mother.'

'Well! I wonder which of the dailies remembered to do that?

We don't have any permanent staff, you see. Just women who come in, one after the other, a stream of them. And they change so often we can't even get used to their faces. Edinburgh used to be a good place for servants, too.'

I could understand that. It had the feel to me of a place which used to be good to have servants in. Maybe the only thing that could see any return to those old days was a lasting depression when servants would become servants again and not expect to go home at nights.

'I don't know what you're getting for a meal,' Ella Baillie said.

I told her I knew. And she liked that. It was easy to get on with her, for the stranger. She didn't seem hunting for the American in me, either, and I was glad. Maybe she'd played golf with a lot of American women and bridge afterwards. They did come over here just to say they'd played the Old Course at St. Andrews, and try some of the newer ones so they could go back to Ohio and tell everyone that the Scots had lost the art of laying out a playable course.

'You might give Sarah a game sometime,' Ella Baillie said. 'She used to play.'

'Not after fifteen, Mother.'

'Not after you started getting ideas about the stage, you mean. What do you think of actresses, young man?'

'I couldn't make any statement without being personal. Sarah's the first one I ever met.'

'I might have guessed that,' Ella said, and laughed. 'But Eileen's got a good grip. She'll be a golfer if she sticks in. She's my younger daughter. She's at school, but holidays start in a fortnight; you'll meet her.'

I had the feeling then of being in as far as this household was concerned, and probably this was what Sarah was thinking, too. She had brought me home on a casual impulse and now I was relaxing in a gilt and damask chair. I could have gone on talking to Ella Baillie for a long time, pretending that I'd come just to do that. I could feel the big woman warming to me, even if I wasn't a golfer.

28

I talked then in answer to direct and interested questions, just giving the answers and no more, not plunging into any monologues. Being an American it wasn't necessary to place me in any social pattern because it was accepted at once that I would be outside anything comprehensible, but she was interested in the make of my car. I nearly told her where a Pontiac came in the scheme of things back home, because somehow I felt sure at once that this would be useful to her. But Sarah took me away to eat.

The dining-room was almost as big as the place with the tiled fire, also draped against the night, not very warm, with a huge table on which were lace mats and wine glasses and steaming tomato soup. Sarah and I sat at one end and there was a bowl of flowers beyond us and silver salt and pepper holders. She passed the toast.

'You certainly were a success upstairs.'

'Ought I to apologize?'

'You can be unpleasant. I'm beginning to think I was wrong about that innocence.'

'I'm just good with people's mums, that's all. It's not a thing you can do anything about. When I cross America by train I'm always buying old ladies their meals in diners.'

'From your great big warm heart?'

'No, I just can't seem to avoid it. Though you may be right in a way. Perhaps I do want people to love me.'

Sarah laughed.

'Well, I'm not going to.'

She took my soup plate away to a little hatch in the wall, opened a sliding door and shouted: 'Mary!' I got up to help with the vegetables and it was self-service from a sideboard. Then we sat down again and I passed the salt but Sarah didn't want any pepper. The fish was all right, but I felt off fish. I was glad of a lager to wash it down.

We ate in what could not be called a companionable silence. The room around us seemed vast and empty, designed for the great days of domestic life when there was always a new face every nine months. All we heard was the invisible Mary singing faintly what sounded like rock an' roll in a Scots accent.

'Ned,' Sarah said carefully. 'I always like to know where I stand. And have other people know, too.'

'Yes?'

'Ned, I won't be seeing you again.'

I looked at her.

'That's a hell of a thing to say to a man before you've given him his dessert.'

Three

WHEN we came out into that hall again after eating I felt that it was the only place in the house that meant anything. It wasn't welcoming but it made a statement. There was even some point in being banished into the night from the hall.

I was almost expecting Sarah to grab my coat and shove me into it, but she was stymied on this by a door opening quite near us. A thin man was watching us, in his fifties somewhere, unmistakably Sarah's father, black hair with white touches for distinction, with Sarah's nose and chin and even her eyebrows. He was extremely neat and wore a dark office suit for late work in his study with a waistcoat tidily buttoned up. There weren't even any creases visible under the Moorish lantern.

'Hello,' he said. 'I was just coming to have coffee with you.'

My feeling was that I hadn't been going to get coffee, but maybe I do the hostess in Sarah an injustice here. Anyway, she made no protest and sure enough a tray was waiting by the fire in the living-room. Mr. Baillie rubbed his hands in there and said:

'Chilly tonight. Dampish, don't you think?'

He wasn't interested in my opinion about the weather. He'd never really bothered to look at me, as though there were only a very few people it was worth his time to inspect. He sat down and filled in all of five minutes lighting a pipe which was obviously in need of maintenance it rarely got. That covered up the time I was getting my coffee and a cigarette.

Mr. Baillie made sucking noises, struck a match, and then through a smelly fog said:

'American, are you?'

It's a mistake for any of us to get tired of our strangeness when we're living out of our own country. After all, it's a point of contact and a starter. I stretched out my legs again, knowing that it was something people didn't do in this setting, and tried to look lanky and amiable. Sarah looked impatient.

But I wasn't in for any questioning this time. The query was merely an opening skirmish and from it Mr. Baillie began to talk with a considerable degree of satisfaction about himself. He was in the building trade, had started in quite a small way, progressed to City Council contracts and was now engaged in the erection of areas of middle-class flats, what he called speculative building, as though there was a lot of building over here where you could calculate your profit before you started.

I must admit it was a little bit of a surprise in that house to have the owner starting off at once to explain how he had got here. I had the impression that Sarah didn't like it, especially when her father began bringing in local big names. Apparently the Lord Provost and the Conservative Councillors and Sir William This were all his pals. Indeed, he was right in. Plainly it was a good thing in the building trade to be able to call the local great by their first names. And having carefully established these gentry with their right titles, Mr. Baillie switched to first names. He almost rubbed my nose in them.

'Ever thought of going in for city politics yourself?' I asked finally.

He looked at me then, suddenly and sharply, as though my intelligence had earned this. Mr. Baillie's pipe fumed; he laughed, and said:

'Funny you should mention that. I'm standing at the elections in May. For a ward in West Edinburgh. The man there is retiring. I have more time now for this sort of thing.'

32

He nearly went on about the citizen's democratic duty to serve in public office but looked at me again and for some reason decided against it. Perhaps he was remembering that I was Sarah's friend, for I could see he was a little nervous now, very conscious of both us, and of a certain hostility from Sarah.

'Like a drink?' he offered, getting up.

From the table where he poured he went on talking. He had an odd voice, thin and slightly high, with a kind of piercing resonance for all the lack of solid power. It sounded like a voice that had gone through a lot of change, perhaps starting out as plain working-class Scots and gradually acquiring a kind of overlay of both gentility and an enlarged vocabulary to which Mr. Baillie had never become quite accustomed. He didn't grope for the word he wanted but accented its arrival so you were bound to notice the achievement.

Sarah was now acting like a daughter whose parent is, from her point of view, showing his worst side, and she definitely wanted to terminate the evening. Mr. Baillie, however, suddenly did not. He came back with the drinks and to his chair and told me about a recent visit to the States in which he had become a great pal of Mr. Harry Schiematz who was apparently a big man in the building business in the new residential areas on the forty-mile fringe out of New York. Mr. Schiematz had gone in for this sort of thing directly from going up to thirty stories in Manhattan apartment houses, and he had transferred modern building techniques to semi-rural areas. It was all very exciting to Mr. Baillie, who was only depressed by Scots conservatism. He wanted to give them sun balconies but they wouldn't take them over here.

I could detect a certain flavour of idealism in all this, at any rate something that would pass for it, in that the profit motive wasn't the only thing which drove Mr. Baillie now. Perhaps he felt that he could relax a little at this point in his career and concern himself with the æsthetics of his form of creation. None the less he hadn't any great feel for the contemporary revival of the Scottish traditional so much in evidence these days. To build in stone in the twentieth century, even to restore, was a waste of new techniques. It wasn't difficult to see Mr. Baillie getting on just terribly well with Mr. Schiematz. And I could imagine Mr. Baillie turned loose in Edinburgh's High Street, with the worn sixteenth-century tenements replaced by clean white cement decorated with chromium strips.

Obviously the hall out there was his wife's taste, not his. He must have hated those deadwood chairs and very often coming into his own house would see it refurbished with indirect lighting and a skin of West African veneer on the walls.

I left about ten. Mr. Baillie had taken his third whisky and was a little flushed. He'd enjoyed talking, so much so that he urged me to come back and listen again. He had a warm place in his heart for all Americans after Mr. Schiematz. There was, said Mr. Baillie, real sympathy and understanding between our two countries, and by that he meant Scotland and America.

In the hall Sarah said:

'Daddy must have had a couple of whiskies with his overtime. I'm sorry, Ned.'

I said it had all been most interesting and for a moment, as I put on my coat, I was quite sure Sarah was taking the trouble to dislike me very much.

Edinburgh is an odd town, your first reaction is physical; you see it with the pleasure that comes from a really brilliant stage set when the curtain goes up for the first time. And when people move in and there is human action you never quite lose that sense of the set dominating the experience played out against it. It didn't strike me as the kind of place you could get emotional about or want again when you had left. I can see it now, on a winter's day; more confined by buildings than Paris, but still open to a tremendous sweep of clean Scots sky, with the wind howling down from the Pentland Hills or coming in from that coldest of northern seas. The colour is firm and set, rarely softened, stone, mostly aged by smoke, the green in the parks all of one tone. Even sunsets follow a pattern, the low-hanging evening mist going purple-mauve in a shade that Hokusai found and used so often.

I had to drive in from Grangemouth along a road that had too much traffic for its width. I'd climb up from the flat lands by the river, leaving behind the glittering plant that meant oil and facing the huge, ancient dumps of slag that meant coal. Scotland's central belt between Edinburgh and Glasgow isn't pretty any more; it isn't even clean. I'll say that for our little city by the river; you mightn't like the sight of great shining cylinders against the hills over the Forth, but at least it wasn't grubby. When you hit the highway you got the smell of the bings, acrid and stinging in your nostrils and the villages you passed through had a kind of dismal Scots permanence.

But Edinburgh sits away from all this. It has a belt of farm land to protect it, then huge areas of suburbs which it ignores, then suddenly the centre of the town, the village street with the gardens and the Castle on one side, the other lined with shops that aim for a note of cosmopolitan sophistication and miss.

I usually got up to town twice a week and now I had a place to go, the Melrose. I kept missing Sarah, but not the others. Angus in particular seemed to have accepted me as a semi-permanent American, and I bought him quite a lot of gins. After about a month he asked me to do a ten-minute spot on radio called 'A Texan looks at Scotland'.

There was quite a bit of trouble about this. I wrote a script timed to my reading capacity, and we found that I managed a third less words in the time than was the norm. Angus worried about this; he took me down to a room in the cellar of Broadcasting House and, sitting me at a desk, conducted me. We managed to get my production rate accelerated a little and another couple of paragraphs squeezed into what I had to say.

Edna came in during the playback in another little cell. She was polite about it; she closed the door and leaned back listening. At the end she said I had a good voice for radio and the three of us went around again to the Melrose which was pretty empty in the early evening.

There Edna and Angus settled in to depress each other. Radio was on its last legs, at least as a cultural medium. Soon the disc jockeys would move in for round-the-clock noise and the behemoth of London Television would swallow up all the money. It was doing it already. Angus had taken cover with his own programme of Scots nostalgia for home and export consumption. He did this once a week with a pile of records and was quite funny about it. He wasn't whimpering, he was just beginning to think about his pension.

I suddenly found myself warming to these two, and it wasn't the gin. They belonged to a small group who had for years put up a fight to maintain a service to five million people. Television reached Scotland in plenty of time for the Coronation of Queen Elizabeth and after that it began to eat them up, slowly at first, then in bigger gulps. Each had their bolt-holes, Angus his records, Edna a job with a repertory company in Glasgow.

'I'm a star,' she said, smiling. 'I get eighteen pounds a week.'

When Angus had to go back to the studios to produce a documentary I took Edna to dinner in the Café Royal. We went downstairs and stood in that state of packed discomfort which seems traditional in popular British pubs, waiting for our turn on a row of stools. Edna had stopped trying with me, and the brittleness had gone, as though she realized that I didn't matter and she could be her forty years.

'Have you gone on seeing Sarah?'

'No.'

'I think she has to be at home a lot. She certainly isn't round and about. But Angus has given her a part in a new adaptation of Galt. A small part. I have the lead. *The Ayrshire Legatees*. Have you read it?'

'No, I never heard of Galt.'

She laughed.

'He was another Scotsman who believed in his bolt-hole. Never trusted himself as a writer. Had to become an engineer or something and make money.'

'I guess that's always been the problem.'

'But he wrote well! And not nearly enough. It makes wonderful radio. We're doing it on Thursday nights, for six weeks. Angus thinks it may be one of the last.'

'What do you mean?'

'Just what we were saying earlier, the whole six weeks will cost about ten minutes of television variety, but that's too much. Can't have that kind of expenditure on old steam. Oh, what the hell! I shouldn't groan, I suppose. The facts are there. Ten years ago we'd have had a quarter-of-a-million listening poll for the Galt. Now it will be about thirty-thousand. Do you believe in polls?'

'We don't use them in my business.'

'We feed on them. Do you know what I thought when I came through that door to listen to your playback? I thought, he'll get eight guineas for this. I could use it. No shame, have I? Why does anyone stay in this bloody game? If I had my time over I'd marry a chartered accountant and live in a nice stone house in the suburbs. Sorry.'

'No need to say sorry. I guess we'd all use our time again differently.'

'You?'

'Sure. As a matter of fact I'd teach. Don't laugh.'

'But you're young! You could . . .'

'Oh, no. The gipsy's seen money in my hand. I'm staying right where I am. Look, can't we eat somewhere quiet with chairs and a table?'

'Upstairs if you want to be grand.'

'Upstairs it is.'

We went out into the street through a revolving door and along the pavement to another door. At once everything was plushier. A man in uniform took my coat and I waited for Edna, sitting on faked antique under a heavily moulded ceiling. A fat old woman came up the stairs wearing yards of mink. Her feet were hurting and she had her face twisted up to keep from moaning.

Edna took her time. When she came out again I saw that she

37

had been subjecting her face to that kind of careful emergency treatment which can take five years off a woman. Her hair had come right, too, and this had done a vast amount for her morale. It was still the same dark suit, tautened up, somehow infinitely smarter. She smiled as though she thought a good evening was starting, and suddenly I had the feeling it might be.

'Turn right,' she said. 'There's more air in this room.'

Again there were high ceilings, gilded this time, gilded mirrors and rosy light. There were stools at a counter, but more tables, all along huge windows. And at the second table from the door, facing me, was Sarah.

She was wearing green in a sharp, clear tone, ear-rings to match, a rounded neckline, and long sleeves. Her make-up was decisive.

'Darling!' said Edna.

'Darling!' said Sarah. 'You know Ralph, don't you?'

Edna did. I was introduced to a young man now on his feet, with reddish hair, reddish moustache, pinky skin and a sturdy frame. His voice meant an expensive education outside Scotland and from this he had a kind of solid poise. He looked at me without interest until he heard the slightly indolent voice which is the only real trace of home I carry around with me, and that seemed to surprise him a little. Then it made him produce a word or two of the polite kindness which the decently bred Britisher keeps for foreigners.

Sarah looked just slightly amused and Edna caught this so quickly that we didn't loiter. I was piloted to a vacant table half-way down the room.

'Ned, if you want to stare at the back of Sarah's neck, you'd better sit in against the window.'

I took that seat. For a minute or two Edna talked fussily about ordering oysters, but her nerve failed her and she went for a shrimp cocktail.

'That's Sarah's solid house in the suburbs,' she told me.

'What does he do?'

'An insurance broker. I've got the feeling he's just about

reached the end of waiting, though. Sarah's got another guess coming if she thinks she can keep him on the hook indefinitely. A man like that reaches a point where he suddenly recovers from youthful folly and starts looking around for the woman who can be the mother of his children. When you've been left a hundred thousand pounds you naturally want to found a dynasty.'

'She might get him to back a play.'

Edna laughed.

'Dear boy, rich young Scots who've inherited only want to increase their holdings without gambling. At the moment Ralph admires the creative in Sarah, but he wouldn't back it with any cash. What he will do is encourage her to go in for amateur drama after the twins have arrived.'

Edna lit a cigarette then, using her own lighter and case so quickly I hadn't time to fumble. She was watching me.

'Ned . . . were you surprised that day when Sarah chased you out of the Melrose?'

'Well, a little, yes.'

'There's always a simple reason for a thing like that. There is this time. From a slight distance you could be her ex-boy friend down in London. I only saw the man once but the resemblance is startling. What was her explanation?'

I looked at Edna.

'She wanted to get away from you all.'

Edna laughed.

'Nonsense. We were making her perfectly at home. Putting ointment on all the sores. Especially Angus. He's particularly good at that. We were welcoming her back.'

'Where she didn't want to be.'

'She *has* talked to you. Somehow that seems very odd. But of course she drinks a lot now. She didn't used to.'

The nice amiable little dinner with Edna wasn't on the schedule any more; we both knew that. Where we were going now wasn't going to be pleasant, but I didn't want to stop.

'What happened with this boy friend?'

39

'Oh, it's the usual. He was a producer beginning to feel his late thirties, with a wife who could never manage to keep her foreign help for the three kids. So she stayed at home and he went out and met Sarah. It happens every day in London and to a lesser extent up here. There's a divorce and a re-marriage, and the second wife finds she can't keep help to look after the new children either. So he starts going out alone again. It's a man's world, of course.'

'In this case there wasn't a divorce?'

'No. Oddly enough. Don't ask me why. Perhaps Sarah got cold feet. It isn't as if she had a religion.'

'By which you mean you're a Catholic?'

Edna smiled at me.

'Aren't you cunning? Yes. And now whenever they need an actress to portray the grim female protester conscience they send for me. I've made what reputation I have being bitterly Presbyterian.'

We had both ordered lobster and it arrived arranged on lettuce, cool-looking and decorated, the red shells a little false, the flesh too delicately pale.

'Potatoes?' the waitress asked.

'No,' Edna said, almost sharply.

The meal they were having down at that other table must have been large and stately. Both Sarah and Ralph were sitting like people who had a lot of eating to get through, with a kind of relaxed attention to the matter in hand. Quantities of food were producing an amiable torpor and I saw her give Ralph the smile of a woman who is bored, but had expected to be, and is not unhappy. It was almost the domesticated companionable boredom of the long-married who have grown used to eating opposite a face.

'I must admit you haven't been doing a lot of staring down in that direction,' Edna said. 'For which I thank you. And now will you allow me to play mum?'

'Advice?'

'Yes. To be an actress, even in Scotland, and even on the radio and in Rep you need a kind of vocation. Sarah doesn't have that. I know. I don't like her, but it's something I look for and respect when I find it. I don't know what she is looking for, I'm not even interested. But I'm perfectly certain of this, it could never be you.'

'Dogmatic, aren't you?'

'Yes, you fool!' she said.

Four

THERE is nothing more unnerving in any room than a portrait in oils of your host or hostess over the mantelpiece. Angus, when young, didn't appeal to me. I'm sure it was a good like-ness, but all one could say in honesty was that he must have been extremely pretty at twenty-five. Now, a quarter of a century later, his face was more comfortably human and, whatever his youth had been, he had come to prefer the pleasures of the table.

'You're looking at that thing,' Angus said. 'It embarrasses me, too.'

We were drinking Madeira.

'I leave it up,' he said, 'for a number of reasons. One of them is that it's a plain statement. It is so easy to forget how thoroughly objectionable one was. Do you like this wine?'

'It's delightful.'

'I've had better, but I like it at this hour. And it's right for a Sunday morning, before the kind of lunch my housekeeper will give you. Are you warm enough there?'

'I'm fine.'

'Do tell me if you're not. There are heaters. One is always a little nervous with Americans. And this room was meant to have two fires in it ... there was a second one on that wall over there. It was completely removed in Victorian times,

42

presumably because you weren't supposed to be comfortable in a drawing-room.'

The room was pure Adam, with a delicate ceiling in moulded plaster, and three windows along one wall which let in the light almost to floor level. Beyond each window was a small, ornamental iron balcony. For my taste the decor was a bit Messel, more fuss than cool space properly decorated with the right piece, but the effect of perfect proportions wasn't lost.

'Have you lived here a long time?'

Carefully Angus poured himself some more wine.

'It was our family house. My father was a surgeon. In those days you lived behind four floors of Georgian frontage. It was converted into flats in the thirties and we kept the best flat. Like fools we sold then, too. If we'd hung on until the forties we'd have made a fortune.'

Angus sipped.

'It's rather odd you should be my guest today. Because as it happens I'm suddenly at the point of crisis. And I need advice from . . . well . . . a neutral.'

When I didn't say anything he smiled at me, as though he thought it seemly that I waited.

'You remember, Ned, how Edna and I got on to the subject of impending doom? For our little world, I mean? Well, just when I was least expecting it I've been offered a new world. It's a bit unnerving. One is made conscious of being in one's fifties. That is the age when the thought of giving up your pension in a gamble is a serious thought.'

'You mean . . . leave the B.B.C.?'

'If I do what I've been asked to do, I shall have to leave the B.B.C. Already I feel almost as though I'd taken the plunge and left the nest. I'm looking back from below somewhere thinking what a comfortable nest it was.'

He was doing nothing of the sort. He was vastly pleased with himself and I became conscious of this suddenly and sharply. Angus was fairly bursting with pleasure at whatever prospects lay just ahead.

'Dear old B.B.C. The great mother. It makes you hesitate

about slamming the door and saying you're on your own. If things weren't changing I don't know that I would. But the thing we've always fought, having Scotland become just another broadcasting region, is something we can't fight any longer. It has happened.'

'You're going over to Commercial Television?'

He didn't like that at all. Butting in on Angus then was like butting in on a Jamesian character, something you couldn't do, you had to wait even though you knew the next five pages weren't going to further the action any. You had to wait, hogtied by sentences, the words dropping on you.

'No, I'm not going over to Commercial Television, Ned. I think I can say I've been offered a better opportunity than that. Much better.'

He had been, too. From what Angus told me it looked at first as though a Scottish bread tycoon had suddenly woken to culture late in life. But as the detail emerged I could see it wasn't quite this; there was a plain commercial proposition involved.

The Scots theatre, such as there is of it, is controlled from London and always has been, but into this picture something new has recently intruded, a vigorous if not very well organized repertory movement. These theatres are professional, but hamstrung for the lack of money, and someone had suggested to the tycoon that the reason they didn't pay better was that they cut themselves off from the people north of the border by looking to England for both players and material. The tycoon had become interested and he was also aware of this new opportunity on TV to sell bread via the drama. A man with a great deal of money, prepared to lose a good deal of it at first, could break the English stranglehold on entertainment, pose as a patriot, and look for profit in the end.

The whole situation only needed centralization and the principles of business efficiency. Glasgow was the place, and in Glasgow had been born, very quietly, a concern known as Scottish Entertainments Ltd., which was preparing to organize and back plays and shows for the theatre, for Commercial

TV, and later to try a hand at films, with even the possibility that the B.B.C. might buy canned drama. Scottish Entertainments Ltd. needed a dramatic director and Angus was it.

With his glass set carefully on a table Angus put his fingers together and talked about opportunity that was also responsibility. Duty came into it, too. It was soon apparent that the suggestion he might seek my advice had been a politeness. Angus, in his mind, had now left his old mum in Broadcasting House and was already right out there in the naughty world. His eyes lifted as he talked and, despite what he said about it, they went towards that portrait in the gilt frame. Youth looked down on Angus in his well-padded chair.

It isn't very often in this life that you get the opportunity of being present at the birth of a man of power, but by a fluke I was in on the ground floor that morning. Already the change was apparent, the producer of radio plays and part-time disc jockey had become a ghost, and in his place was a tycoon's right-hand man.

'I've always wanted to stay in Scotland, Ned. I've put that first. Oh, I know in many ways that was folly. In London I would have been given scope that I could never hope to get up here. But I wouldn't go. Now it is as though a wheel has turned, and the impossible has come up.'

Obviously destiny had been hard at work on a long-term project with Angus, and it was only now that the vast pattern was beginning to make itself plain to his eyes. He saw the beauty of the whole design but was not dazzled by it.

'Is the money really good?' I asked.

He looked at me, for a moment startled. Then he relaxed.

'Ah . . . a sensible question. Yes, it is. Very good indeed. And I don't even have to live in Glasgow. I wouldn't say this to many, but I simply couldn't. However, I can commute, which is a great thing. My settled little world here won't be upset.'

No need to take the portrait off its hook. I was ready for my lunch.

The dining-room in the flat was half an apartment of pleasing proportions sliced in two by a breezeboard partition and the result was weird in the extreme. You ate in an upended box, with the ceiling a long way off, but the walls pressing in. The furnishings were Scottish mahogany 1880, painful to look at and sit on, and our food was served on enormous pieces of porcelain with a dismal blue design, mostly worn off, on a white background. There was a soup tureen and ladle, and when it was time for the second course the door was kicked open.

In came a tall, angular woman in a black dress which I immediately labelled bombazine, though I haven't the faintest idea what that is. At any rate it was slightly shiny and stiff and there was a creaking that might have been the material or corsets.

The joint was put in front of Angus, a medium-size sirloin roast, but on a platter so vast the meat looked lost and the browned potatoes seemed to huddle in against the cold. There was also creamed cauliflower, under a lid, and horseradish sauce.

The woman never looked at me. There was no deference towards the guest or feeling for a slight occasion about this. She just didn't look, aggressively, and for a moment I had a slight uneasiness at the thought that there could be a history in this house of people having meals towards whom black bombazine had felt the sharpest disapproval.

She was a character Angus told me, as he carved the meat, a girl taken into his father's service, faithful to his mother, and then handed on to him.

'I don't think she lives in this world at all, Ned, otherwise I wouldn't have her. When I think what I pay her and what she could get if she wanted to . . . well, I don't think about it. I couldn't imagine this flat without Agnes.'

The meat was excellent and so was the Beaujolais we drank with it. Then came the usual dreaded anticlimax of British eating, what they rightly call pudding, ground rice and sour plums. After that we went back to the Georgian splendours.

46

I had accepted this invitation largely because of the second part of it, which was that we go on to a rehearsal of Angus's new production of the serialized Galt story where I knew I was bound to see Sarah. This started at four. It was now quarter past two. Angus settled in with coffee and then whisky to pass the time by telling me about himself.

Most of British reticence is merely caution, they want to talk about themselves as much as we do, but a longer history of the results of indiscretion make them observe certain rituals before they make use of you. However, when you have been fed and wined and are surrounded by your host's possessions you are then as much threatened by his private life as you would be by an American middle-aged matron's in a Pullman.

Angus was in a philosophical frame of mind, the sort of thing that hits a lot of people with the news that they are moving into the money. He began by telling me why he had never married, which seemed unnecessary, but not to him.

'I know what you must have thought, Ned, when you first met me. Let me say in a little preface that how I go about the world is partly a convenience. If you seem to fit into a classification, you are less menaced by the norm. Even women begin to be patronizing, and a patronizing woman is the only one who isn't dangerous to your security. I dislike the norm, I always have. It seemed to me a sell. Perhaps I was never quite young, for I can remember that at twenty I was sure marriage was something I didn't want. In our time if you show you don't want the norm the psychiatrist boys find a label for you and, though you may buck the label for a bit, you come to see that the most sensible thing to do is to accept it. It gives you your immunity card and that saves a vast amount of bother all around.'

Angus looked at his whisky. I was feeling very heavily settled in my chair.

'I'm not really concerned that you should believe this, but it happens to be true. I'm not very interested in women physically, but neither am I interested in my own sex. I'm one

47

of nature's bachelor uncles. But they're out of fashion so I play up to the immunity card.'

I felt this was too soon after ground rice and plums but there was nothing I could do. The ormolu clock under the portrait was cynically slow.

'I've said that for me marriage seemed a sell. You know, I think it is for a very much larger proportion of men and women than is generally admitted. I'm in my fifties now and I have that solid body of people I've known for twenty, even thirty, years. I can see two, possibly three, marriages in which I believe the partners are essential to each other and have grown more so as time went on. With the rest it looks more like an endurance contest. In the houses of most of my married friends there isn't even much effort made to disguise a chronic state of suspended boredom. In these cases the only thing that I can see to be maintaining the union is complete inertia on both sides. Children, of course, bring a massive obligation and make the picture fuller, but not any prettier. I abominate the complete hopelessness which leads parents to abrogate their private and personal living in favour of a generation to come. These accept failure in their own lives with a dismal, philosophic calm, and the only thing that can brighten their eyes is the contemplation of a future for their young. And, of course, their children grow up to hate them.'

'Oh,' I said. 'Sure of that?'

'Absolutely. I was my parents' hope, the only one as it happened. It's an unbearable imposition on any child. It only breeds the kind of bitterness from which it may take you years to escape.'

'You're against marriage?'

'No, I'm against the institution. I'm convinced that marriage is only successful between the aggressive and I had the sense to realize early that I wasn't aggressive enough to make a success of it. My poor wife, whoever she might have been, is almost certainly a little better off with her suburban Civil Servant.'

I could agree with him there.

'You're wondering where you come in to all this, Ned?'

48

I had been, distantly, but with the knowledge that there is always something for you in anything that anyone else wants to say at considerable length.

'Ned, I know you won't mind my saying this, but you're woman hunting. And you're the kind to sentimentalize your lusts. You want them consecrated. Or, if not quite that, you want a woman as a stabilizing factor in your life. I think this is inviting disaster. Of course, you're at perfectly liberty to take a look at my waistcoat and decide that I'm producing a theory to comfort my own isolation. About that I'd only say one thing. I'm a terribly happy man!'

He was, too. A portrait, and an Adam room, a cook, and now all the heavens opening. He looked up at them beyond the wrought plaster and then over to the boy with the tight little smile.

'Freedom, Ned, is the ability to move where you like without being tied to considering others. This is freedom at forty or fifty or sixty, even though at thirty it may be hard to believe. You have that freedom now. Don't throw it away carelessly.'

Usually my stomach can take anything, but just then an enormous ball of wind moved up and started to press on my heart, setting up palpitations. On the way out I found what I wanted in the bathroom, bicarbonate of soda under a trade name.

Not many of us know how to use our big moments, they catch us unawares and we muff them, very often speechless. But not Angus.

He told me when we were outside the rehearsal studio that he had a thing about people watching him produce, and that if I didn't mind he'd ask me to sit well back from everyone. Then we pushed open two doors with port-holes in them and went into a large hall which clearly could be used to house a live audience when those noises were wanted. Now it was as empty, even of chairs, as a ballroom in the hands of the cleaners, and, though there must have been fifteen people waiting for Angus, they were all grouped up at one end, forming an odd, static and curiously silent tableau of bored patience. The girls were in slacks, except Edna, and the men in sweaters or battered sports jackets. Sarah was sitting on the edge of a low platform, one knee up, her hands on it, and her chin on her hands. She didn't see us come in, but a sort of general muttering that might have been a greeting for Angus made her look up. She lifted a hand and pushed back her black hair, then picked up a script from the boards of the platform.

Sarah's movement was all part of a general rustling to attention that only pretended to be casual. Angus, before advancing on them, gave me one last look and a wave of his hand.

'Somewhere over there, Ned.'

There was one chair over against a padded wall and I went to it with the feeling that Angus had taken the trouble to tell someone where he wanted that chair. I was at least thirty feet from the actors and sat down without anyone taking any notice of me at all. Angus might have come in alone. Sarah never looked at me, nor did Edna for that matter. They were all looking at Angus.

For nearly two hours I watched a producer at work for the first time. And I was impressed by his complete command, for one thing. He was in no way one of the gang; he had a script which he was interpreting, using the available actors. It was as simple as that, indeed there was a visible ruthlessness about Angus now, an edge on his voice sometimes, and he didn't call anybody Darling.

The adaptation was in what I suppose could be called period Scots, and Ayrshire Scots at that, but I got a lot of it, I think nearly all, and despite the almost continuous interruptions from Angus I could see a pattern of satire emerging that was sharp and intelligent.

Angus appeared completely absorbed, he was often the actor himself, taking someone's lines to give them back again with a kind of reluctance. And he was a lot better than most. It seemed to me that when he attacked Sarah's part he was better than she. Sarah watched him with a kind of painful intensity, nodding her head, and then doing what he told her not quite so well.

I suppose all producers could have been actors and many of them have been. Possibly it was the actor in Angus which made him so ponderously dull when he tried to be original. Earlier this afternoon in his solo performance for me he had made two mistakes, first in miscasting himself as the bland observer, and second in writing his own lines. Now when he had someone else's good lines to use he knew what he was about.

The rehearsal came to a very abrupt end. Angus simply said that would do now. He seemed tired and went to sit on the edge of the platform and for a moment or two there was a sort of chattering amongst the actors. Angus pulled out a handkerchief and patted his forehead but when someone offered him a cigarette he shook his head. He said suddenly, in a voice that studio padding didn't soften:

'I've something to tell you all. I won't, after all, be doing the Galt. Rory MacKindrick is taking over.'

For a moment there was complete silence, then Edna called out:

'Rory? Doing the Galt? But he's variety!'

Angus's head came up, slowly. He was smiling slightly.

'Rory has stood in for me before.'

'Angus, you can't do this! Not to the Galt. If you've got to go to London or something, then hold it over. Rory, of all people. He'll thump through it.'

'You're a little unkind, Edna. And I'm afraid you're going to have to get used to Rory. I think, you see, that he's certain to be my successor.'

The timing for that had been quite perfect. He had their attention in exactly the way he wanted it and he gave them his news gently, with strong overtones of regret. Still, everything was made perfectly plain, Angus was on the way out and up.

It should all have been anticlimax to me, but it wasn't. I mightn't have been there in my chair against the wall in those moments when everyone in that room, except Angus and me, was trying to assess what this change was going to mean. They were already uneasy enough in their little world, but this was an earthquake, the jolt of disaster. If a variety producer was taking over drama there was more than a smell of high policy behind the move. It almost certainly meant thin times for the actor who couldn't sing, or yodel, or try his hand as feed to some established Scottish comic.

Edna had been listening with her hands down at her sides, her fingers folded into fists. Now suddenly, in one swift movement, she brought her hands up to her face and covered it. The gesture would have been too heavily dramatic in another place, but it wasn't here. It did more than underline a general bewilderment, it was personal, but for them all, a woman for a moment not wanting to look at a thing which had yawned open at her feet.

Angus made a little sound that seemed to be a clearing of his throat.

'I hope you all realize,' he said, 'that this is going to mean opportunity for the lot of you.'

Edna's hands dropped.

'My dear, there's no need to stare at me like that. Don't you see? For the first time in my life I'm going to be in a position to do something about the drama in Scotland, not just take my instructions from someone else.'

'Do, Angus? What are your plans? Are you going to replace the singing commercials with five-minute playlets advertising soap?'

He stood.

'You don't have to take that line! You ought to know me well enough to be certain that I wouldn't go to a job like that.'

'Oh, hell!' Edna said.

I think Angus felt then that the situation was getting a little out of hand. He produced a case, lit himself a cigarette, and then looked beyond Edna.

'Let me tell you this. I haven't just jumped into this thing. I checked up very carefully indeed on what was planned for now and the future. I can tell you that the man behind all this is really concerned with the theatre in Scotland.'

'He makes a stinking awful bread,' an actor said.

Angus moved his body.

'We're going to produce more plays in one form or another than have ever been produced in Scotland before.'

He didn't add that the man in control was going to be Angus. He didn't need to. They had got that now, and uneasiness drove them into silence. They all seemed to be waiting for a move from someone, and Edna made it. She turned and found a bag on the stage. I noticed she was wearing the same suit she had tightened up for dinner with me. She tucked the bag under her arm and began to walk down the studio.

'Edna!'

She turned.

'I'm sorry, Angus. You know I don't throw temperament very often. I've never been able to afford to. But I simply can't do the Galt under Rory MacKindrick, and that's all there is to it. Why in heaven's name couldn't you have waited until this production was over?'

'I had to take this appointment at once.'

'I see. Even with your bread king you're not quite free. Oh, I'm sorry, Angus. I shouldn't have said that. I suppose in a month or so I'll come to you and apologize. I hope you'll let me.'

Edna walked on down the studio, stealing the scene, and the doors with the port-holes swung shut behind her.

I hadn't been watching Sarah. Now I looked for her, and saw her folding her script very neatly and sliding it into a pocket of her slacks. Over one arm hung a duffel-coat. She went up to Angus.

'Edna's tired just now. She has a heavy part in Glasgow. I don't think she meant what she said, Angus. She hadn't had time to think about what this means. For me . . . well, I'm glad you have this chance. I know you're going to make an awful lot of it.'

'Thanks, dear.'

Sarah had started up the action again after a too effective exit had stopped it. And the others fell back on their training then and moved in. Angus was surrounded. In a moment or two there was even laughter. I held open the door for Sarah and as she went through it she looked straight at me and smiled.

'Hello,' she said.

In the corridor we were quite alone.

'You have a face, Ned dear, which cries out for you. Didn't you enjoy watching us?'

'Not the last scene.'

Sarah laughed.

'All right, I'm a bitch. Old Angus is right up there now. Allah, Allah, salaam. If you were going to offer me a lift in your lovely car, I've got my pappy's Daimler.'

'Sarah, I'd like to see you for a little. Isn't there some place we can go?'

'You ought to know by this time that there's no place you can go in Edinburgh on a Sunday except an hotel lounge, and I don't feel like that. I don't feel like asking you home for supper either, though Mother would like to talk to you.'

'Your mother?'

'Yes, dear. In spite of all my protests that I haven't seen you to speak to since you were last in her company, she's absolutely convinced we're having an affair. Good night.'

Sarah went down into Queen Street and for a little I was undecided about whether I ought to go back and say a word to Angus. Then the slightly suspicious look of the porter at an unauthorized person loitering in those precincts made me move on out after Sarah into the rain. She was just backing out the Daimler and I could see her clearly from the dashboard lights. She smiled and waved at me.

Five

I'D been too long on that commuters' run to Edinburgh to notice anything but the traffic on the route until the Sunday morning a week after Angus's lunch and rehearsal. I had to get to the big west end hotel by eleven and I hit the streets of the city centre just about church time, and all at once something was defined again, the clanging of bells coming right into the car through the closed windows.

In Abilene I'd been a regular attender, and when I went home it was assumed that I still was wherever I might be. The fact that this didn't happen to be the case any more wasn't ever rebuked in the cities where I found myself. But suddenly in Edinburgh I felt caught, an American in a brightly painted car, riding when almost everyone else was on foot. I rolled down the driving window to catch a blast of damp cold and the full volume of those bells. Between them were little cracks of silence in which there was no roar of traffic at all, but only the shuffling of feet. The roads were almost empty but on all the pavements were little family groups going to church, a lot of the boys in the kilt.

Oddly enough those kilts were almost the only colour, the rest a grey background with dark figures moving against it, even the women sombre, clutching black hymn books and Bibles.

Those bells clashing amongst the gloomy stone buildings! It didn't have the small town Sunday feeling of home at all, the sense of altered tempo you get, of a church at the corner suddenly again the focal point, with the leafy streets stretching away, and the lawns kept green by a lot of watering and the parked cars, bright as mine, right away as far as you could see. I was suddenly conscious of how much this had the edge on us for solemnity. This was God's day, and without that suggestion of a specially large dinner waiting after the duty of worship. Maybe those women out there were thinking about whether they'd set the oven controls to the right point, but they didn't look like it. They walked subservient to their men, most of whom had the incredible period dignity of almost black suits and bowler hats.

I parked my car in Charlotte Square and got out into the noise of those bells calling all sinners. A steady file of people were climbing up to the façade of the huge Adam church and disappearing amongst the columns, and I had to walk in the other direction, worldly in my too bright tweed coat. I thought about the preaching I was missing, the habit of subjecting yourself to the weekly admonition which was perhaps, after all, a kind of spiritual discipline. At any rate that's how I had been taught to think about it through a lot of years. Maybe it was the cumulative effect of a great many sermons in my past, but right then I wanted to turn and go in with those people, to take a hymn book from the hands of a solemn looking elder who wouldn't smile at me. I wanted to stand with a lot of others and sing the hymns I knew I'd recognize.

It was a weakening surge of feeling to have hit you just before you went into a hotel to see Harry Bidacker.

The revolving doors shut out the bells. In the lobby was a smell of perfumed disinfectant, expensive cooking and somewhere a bit of redecorating going on. The carpets were very thick and the girls behind the reception desk carefully made up for the new day on principles laid down by one of the international goddesses of beauty, which meant that there wasn't any way you could really tell what they looked like.

'Yes, sir?' said a cushioned, Scots-Hollywood voice. 'Can I help you?'

'I'm calling to see Mr. Harry Bidacker.'

'Just a moment please, I'll see if he's in his suite.'

She telephoned. The fixed smile stayed on her lips.

'Yes, Mr. Bidacker. Certainly, Mr. Bidacker.' Then to me. 'Mr. Bidacker wonders if you'll wait for him in the lounge?'

I went into the lounge and sat down and began to think about Harry Bidacker. And I started to feel just a little scared as I thought about him.

The company I work for operates all over the world and in many places it establishes its own little towns. When you live in one of these you're conscious that big brother, benevolent but sharp-eyed, is doing a lot of watching. Right now, with a handful of others, I was outside one of these spheres of organized company influence, rather alone in the big world, but that didn't mean the watching had ceased. Harry had just flown over to Prestwick as a reminder that the watching never really ceased at all.

I'd met Harry Bidacker about half a dozen times and always he'd hit me on the back, called me Ned, and given me a big smile. He was a personnel manager. His job was to keep tabs on the sheep who had temporary appointments outside the fold.

Harry kept me waiting, and I don't think that was policy, only that he was late in getting up after a long air flight. But when he came into the lounge, that Sunday morning was his; he claimed it with the kind of smile that tends to settle on a man when his earnings have moved well above twenty-five thousand dollars a year.

'Ned! Well, it's good to see you!'

Harry was a big man, wearing a two hundred and fifty dollar suiting which had still been plucked off a hanger and didn't fit him. He looked like a man who had slipped into someone else's jacket by mistake, an even bigger man than he was. But perhaps he was leaving room for development. He thumped me on the back.

'How you doing, Ned? Here, let's sit down. We can have some coffee, though I don't recommend it. Would you rather have a drink?'

I was already wary, I took coffee. Harry sat back, his glasses glinting a little, and told me about the flight over the Atlantic which was easily the worst he'd ever had, with electric storms, both going up and coming down, something the pilot hadn't experienced in ten years.

'I always bring bad weather in airplanes, Ned. It's a wonder to me I haven't been killed long ago. Well now, how are you getting on at that little Scotch town of yours?'

'Oh, fine. Of course there aren't many of us now. Just really the six families and me and Tommy Baines.'

'How's Tommy? How's he making out with those Scotch lassies, eh?'

'He never tells me a thing, Harry.'

'Aren't you two living together any more?'

'No . . . I . . . ah, got a tip about some new lodgings. The hotel wasn't so good. I moved in with a very nice couple who rent me their garage. Tommy stayed on in the hotel.'

'Oh,' said Harry.

He didn't like that, he didn't like the boys splitting up, not when there were so few Americans in the place.

'You and Tommy see a good deal of each other, Ned?'

'Oh, sure, around, you know.'

'Well now, I guess you're glad to be living near a city like Edinburgh. You'll be in here a lot? Not much to do in that Grangemouth, I suppose?'

'Not a great deal.'

'So you make for here?'

Glasses glinted and the smile stayed while the waiter brought coffee and poured it and Harry said it looked like some kind of molasses. He made a face as he sipped and before he over-tipped the waiter.

'I don't know how you can do it,' he said to the man, 'unless you're using old coffee grounds. Making good coffee is just so elementary. However, here you are. . . .'

The man didn't like us. A couple of damned Yanks in the middle of his morning.

'Well,' said Harry, lighting a cigarette. 'You know why

I'm here, Ned. Oh, I must tell you a new one straight from
the Board Meeting. I'd been called in and gave them a brief
résumé of my new programme. And after it old Sam Widem-
shein looked up and said: "There goes our Hermes again."
So I'm Hermes now, a little overweight, maybe.'

I laughed and Harry shook in his chair.

'Ned, I hear you got on the radio?'

How the devil had he heard that?

'It wasn't much, Harry, just a few minutes. Sort of im-
pressions.'

'Sure, I know. A Texan looks at Scotland. You know, when
I heard about it I thought that was a good idea. It shows a
degree of integration.'

'I . . . ah . . . don't quite follow?'

'Oh, it's simple enough! Integration. That's what we want,
one of the things. It's something we look for in our men
abroad. It's a measure of their adaptability. You know, it's
taken us Americans a long time to realize that we have to
become citizens of the world . . . as well as Americans. A
concern like ours isn't just an international business, every
member of the team has a social function in terms of the community in which he lives as well. You know what we're
accused of, building little Americas wherever we go. Well, that
is not the policy of the firm for which you and I are both
working. We're turning our eyes to the horizons beyond and
thinking not only in terms of the product we offer.'

There was a pause. I was getting the sermon I'd half wanted.
It was a solemn moment. Harry had a lot to say and he said it
with the kind of earnestness which was almost a statement that
he had been given a salary raise before he left the States.
Personnel Management was now something that took part in
those Board Meetings right up at the top. Harry was, in fact,
someone to be afraid of.

'Ned, I'm very interested in your approach to living abroad.
It may not seem in a job of temporary duration of this kind
that there is any point in much contact with the local people.
But that's a mistaken attitude. It is of vital importance to each

and every one of us, wherever we go, to establish very real and sincere contacts with the civic and business leaders of that community.'

I was beginning to get the point of the sermon, the text even. It lay in that mention of civic and business leaders.

'That's why I thought your radio talk was a good idea, Ned. It gets your name about. It makes people ask . . . who is this man? It's a step in the right direction. It's a step, too, that I'm sure you have followed up.'

He looked at me, very hard, then. He even paused to allow me at this point to insert a few names of business and civic leaders. I hadn't even one to give him from something I'd read in the newspapers.

Wait a minute! Mr. Baillie, the building magnate. The man who had been in New York and liked chromium. That was a name all right. I looked modest, at the floor.

'Scotland is a conservative country,' I said. 'They don't rush at you.'

'Oh, we know that, Ned. But I can see you have something up your sleeve, that you haven't been wasting your time. A young man like you? I'm sure that contacts are there all right, and one or two of them might just be by a pretty daughter.'

How right he was, how very right. I gave him the smile of an irrepressible American boy. Harry loved it.

I thought of Sarah just then, and her 'Allah, Allah, salaam'.

Grangemouth is almost a boom town with the oil refineries, but the part I drove to had been built before the war, and it looked like something you see attached to every Scots city, a pattern of little houses which for sheer geometric ugliness of design and placing beat anything you can find in two hemispheres. This particular suburb, more than twenty-five years old, had some growth in the gardens, some green, but even here were the patterns still, the sharp angles of grass and what would be, in summer, flower beds. Every house had a bay-window on the left side of the front door and a double window on the right. You went up a concrete walk and in the plywood door, usually painted brown, was a sagging moon of a bevelled glass window letting light into the hall beyond.

The house I chose was called Tomanna, and before I pushed the bell I heard screams from inside, in strong American accents. Three kids opened the door. They were Joey, Isabel and Mary-Anne. They poured over me and passed, but Mary-Anne tripped on a bicycle and hit the concrete. The noise suddenly had a solo treble piercing through it.

'Joey!' Gracie called out. 'Pick her up! And if it's the butcher's van, I'm just coming.'

'It's only Uncle Ned,' I said.

Gracie was in the kitchen, her blonde hair not exactly organized, her frilled, American gingham apron not as fresh-looking as the frilled fuss curtains over the sink. She had eaten off her lipstick.

'What do you want?' Gracie asked. 'If it's Joe, he's not here.'

'I know where Joe is; he's in Edinburgh being probed by Harry Bidacker.'

'You're wrong. Joe is the last on the list. He doesn't go in until tomorrow. He's at the works. Naturally. I can see us all in Tahiti, building a refinery on an atoll. There are waving palms, and sound track music and a great yellow moon. Joe will be at the works. Do you know, I sit down and try to remember just when it was that Joe took time off to assist in conceiving his children.'

'I'm an unmarried man, Gracie.'

'Even then you should have enough sense not to come and see me at this time of day. What's the matter? Have you come here to warn us that Mr. Bidacker is hunting for Red Americans in Scotland?'

'No, we're being integrated.'

'What? There's some sherry in the living-room. Let's go. Joey! What have you done with Mary-Anne?'

At the door to that tiny front parlour Gracie paused.

'Oh, hell,' she said. 'I forgot about the "thing". Oh, well, it doesn't matter. Come in.'

The house was rented furnished. There was plenty of furniture in the room, what we used to call an overstuffed suite, and it was. There was a fire on in a tiny fire-place, mostly smouldering black coal and in the clear area in front of this was a vast wooden packing case, with straw strewn out from it on to one of those hearth-rugs that had been someone's hobby for six years of winter evenings.

'That is the "thing",' Gracie said. 'It's the biggest mixer in the world. Try and lift it. From my mother. As soon as she heard we had electricity over here in Scotland she started to send me all the things that the American housewife can't live without. It's no use telling her I can. I've written, I've even cabled, and once we were on the phone at twelve dollars for two minutes. It's no good. They keep coming. I'm expecting a king-size refrigerator soon, you know the sort, where you can keep a whole ox in deep freeze in a bottom drawer. I'm terrified!'

I poured the sherry. Gracie found a bag and a lipstick. Very carefully she shaped her mouth.

'Gracie, I've come here to talk to you seriously.'

'It's years since anyone's done that. You might as well sit down.'

I sat down and looked at her.

'You're the most intelligent woman in our little community.'

She smiled, thought about it, and then withdrew the smile.

'I'd call that a qualified compliment, but carry on. Though I ought to go and see what's happened to Mary-Anne.'

'The noise has stopped.'

'That probably means they're all three lying under the baker's van waiting for the nice man to start the engine. Is it something to do with this Bidacker?'

'Yes. He wants to give a monster cocktail party at the company's expense in the biggest hotel to the people we've integrated with.'

'What? But Joe and I haven't integrated at all. The only thing Joe could possibly have in common with another human being is an engine. He married me because I started early on in our contact to say: "Fix it".'

'Gracie, this is serious. We're all of us caught. We haven't any important contacts.'

'Well, why the hell should we? You men are paid to do a job.'

'Business is not simple any more. We're all little ambassadors of the American way.'

'I'm not. I refuse to be! I think we all clutter our lives with too damn' much equipment. I've never wanted a Cadillac from the time I was a little girl and though that may be a terribly un-American thing to say, it's the truth. I was also born totally devoid of charm.'

'Nonsense, I'd marry you like a shot if it weren't for Joe.'

'Why let that stop us these days? But I guess Joe's three kids would be a frightful psychological complication to our future happiness. Are you a romantic man?'

'Well, I was told the other day that I want to dress up my lusts.'

Gracie looked delighted.

'Really? Ned, dear, I always thought you were perfectly normal. You see, it just shows. I'm not even perceptive.'

'Gracie, about this cocktail party. I'm working on a line that may be productive. I think I can do a round-up of the sort of people that Bidacker has in mind. But we're going to need a lot. And I remembered about your car crash.'

'Don't!'

'Look, I have a reason. You hit the back of a Bentley, and in that Bentley was a man called Sir Roger Strathlaird.'

Gracie looked decidedly hostile.

'Why drag all this up? Joe does it every second night.'

'I've got a reason. This man Sir Roger was pretty amiable, wasn't he?'

'Well, I was a helpless female driving alone and he was a gentleman. Oh, Ned, he was! He was perfectly sweet. He had on a hairy suit and a hairy cap to match and he only shaved so far up his cheeks so there was hair under his eyes as well as above. I adored him and I must have shown it. But I won't allow you to make use of him.'

'The point is, you did go to his house, didn't you?'

'We did, a couple of days later, Joe and I. To fix things up without insurance. It was a huge house in acres of grounds and there was absolutely no heat and we ate cold scones.'

'Sir Roger Strathlaird,' I said, 'is the Deputy Lord Lieutenant of his county. I looked him up.'

'I can well believe it. And what is a Deputy Lord Lieutenant?'

'He's the Number Two man. When the Number One is sick, your Sir Roger meets the Queen's train and helps her on and off it.'

'Good heavens!' Gracie said.

There was a considerable silence while Gracie thought about this. Then she said:

'The answer is no. If you think I'm going to make use of something that happened to me out of the blue in order to catch a lion for this Bidacker's cocktail party, you can just think again.'

'It's our cocktail party, and our futures, dearie. Have you ever heard what French wives do for their men?'

'I've got a feeling I'm going to be embarrassed in a minute. But I thought the respectable ones just held the purse strings?'

'They build a world for their husbands. From the moment of marriage his future is her future. They create the kind of social setting that will promote his advancement.'

'I never promised to do anything like that for Joe. Besides, he wouldn't realize I was doing it. The answer is still no.'

'All you've got to do is send them a card, telling them that Harry Bidacker will be "At Home" in a hotel suite. You add a little note on the back from one accident victim to another. It's up to the Deputy Lord Lieutenant and his wife whether or not they accept. You never know, we might be lucky. That card might arrive on a secret "be kind to Americans week". You find that every now and then the British get conscience smitten about the transatlantic cousins living in their midst.

64

If it hadn't been for your accent, Gracie, you'd have never been asked home for that cold scone.'

'What do you mean?'

'I mean that you are right outside the local social system and so the Deputy L.L. could risk offering you the kind of politeness he'd serve up to a visiting Chief from Basutoland in one of those striped nighties.'

'You're making me feel an object.'

'But that's the secret of success for us over here, Gracie. Once we accept the fact that we're objects, the whole temperaature gets ten degrees warmer. Go on, gamble on it. You've nothing to lose and think of a real Sir to go with the Martinis. Harry Bidacker has taken the Peacock Room for a week next Tuesday. He'll be back from Holland then on his way to Mexico. Please, Gracie.'

'You're a snake,' she said.

Six

JAMES BAILLIE came out of the inner office to meet me. He was even neater-looking than he had been at home, everything about him pressed and starched, and the excessive dapperness in some way underlined the fact that he wasn't a very tall man. I seemed a long way above him.

'This is just cheek, Mr. Baillie, barging in right in the middle of your morning.'

'Not at all, not at all. It's just as I told you on the phone, I always have a cup of coffee at this time. Jennie always brings it in to me, don't you, Jennie?'

Jennie was in her early forties with the kind of figure that seemed to pout over the top of her steel desk. She had a bright cheerful face, and had been aiming to please for at least a quarter of a century.

'Yes, that's quite true. Mr. Baillie always has his coffee at this time.'

I got coffee, too, made from milk and a tin can, and there was a round tea biscuit. Mr. Baillie munched his with the briskness of an executive who knows the body has to be maintained. He watched me all the time and even with the biscuit in his mouth there was the hint of a Dale Carnegie smile in front of it, something worn during business hours for interviews.

'I have a problem,' I said. 'And you're the only one I can think of to help me.'

He liked that; I knew he would. I'll go far in my profession. I may even reach the second layer from the top.

'The thing is this, Mr. Baillie, one of the major executives of my company has just arrived in Europe. I think this is his first trip to Scotland, and you know how we're placed out there at Grangemouth; we're really just technicians doing a job and liable to be moved somewhere else at any time. That doesn't give one the lead towards the sort of contacts one might desire in a community. The visit of Mr. Bidacker has pointed this up sharply for me. I realize that though I've thoroughly enjoyed my time in Scotland I've been neglecting certain opportunities in this country.'

Mr. Baillie moved perceptibly in his chair, the movement was slightly towards me. He moistened his lips. The biscuit had gone and the smile had settled.

'Naturally men like Mr. Bidacker are interested in the creative side of business, in the men who control policy. They're the kind of people he wants to meet in this world that is every day getting smaller and smaller. Only the other morning he said to me . . . "Ned, we American businessmen have got to integrate with our opposite numbers in the free democratic countries. We've got to get to know these people and be on friendly working terms with them." And I agree with these sentiments, Mr. Baillie. I can assure you, I'm a long way from being an executive. . . .'

I nearly said 'yet' but was glad I hadn't when I saw that Mr. Baillie appreciated the omission. In fact, Mr. Baillie was right with me. He knew all about my company. Off-hand he could have probably told me our registered capital, if it is registered, which I rather doubt with the American laws against combines.

Everything began to work out just as I'd hoped. There wasn't a Rotary lunch he could take me to that morning, but something almost as good; Mr. Baillie was a member of a club in Edinburgh where in the middle of the day the local citizens who were there, and going further, assembled to eat a slightly worse meal than they'd have got in one of the Princes

Street tea-shops. At ten minutes to one I walked through these portals with Mr. Baillie and the introductions started almost at once.

I was pleased to find him selective about this, as though he had an easy reference file in his mind which he kept continually bringing up to date. I heard quite a few potted biographies, all with the smell of money, and more than that, the thing we like best, a fight to get it. These were the warriors, without a silver spoon amongst them, at least not on the list offered me. I never heard an English accent nor got a hint of any intrusion of the public school trade union into these premises.

By two-fifteen I'd met the man who according to Mr. Baillie was going to be the next Lord Provost of Edinburgh and received an invitation to visit the City Chambers. That was nice for a touch of the formal, but much more important was a suggestion that I visit the costing department of a chain of multiple stores, look at a new building scheme going up for the town council under contract with the largest construction company north of the border, and see how Scottish Insurance really worked, whatever that might mean; and finally twenty men, middle-aged men, who didn't drive their own cars any more, knew what an invitation to meet Harry Bidacker was all about.

We might have been in Altoona. It was suddenly very plain to me why something like eighty per cent of American capital investment in Britain since the war has been located in Scotland. They were more formal about their Sundays, but this was home. They even had their own version of the log cabin— over here, a croft in the mountains where you grew up eating porridge and sleeping on heather. None of the men I met that morning looked like they'd ever slept on heather, but it's a nice thing to have in your national tradition. I went out from that club into the rain practically starry-eyed and with me went an echo of James Baillie's voice saying: 'He's the principal director of a big business. A very, *very*, big business.'

It's impossible for an American with any normal American

instincts at all not to love a bunch of Scotsmen who have got on.

Sarah Baillie showed up at the cocktail party in the Peacock Room. She had been included in the invitation, but I certainly didn't expect to see her.

She walked in with her father. There were already about thirty people in the room, which had heavy brocaded curtains drawn, gilded furniture and a purple carpet. Waiters in white jackets had trays of glasses, and there was that subdued roar which meant the second cocktail down and the third just coming up.

Sarah was wearing black. It was tight just below her knees and then it loosened and sort of flowed upwards. It was a dress which had no positive shape but it might have been designed in Italy to reveal the shape beneath, whenever a girl made the slightest movement. It was sexy in the way French clothes never are, and British clothes wouldn't dream of attempting.

For that evening Sarah was not a Scottish lassie. This would have clicked even with Harry Bidacker, indeed it did click, and he was over in a minute, holding Sarah's hand between his own two well-manicured hams.

He wasn't quite as extrovert as I'd expected. Travel had done something for Harry; there were things he'd come to recognize; he'd evolved a kind of polish unusual in the oil business. Sarah even listened to him. Once she looked at him, as if she saw him.

Then she looked at me.

'Hello, darling.'

Oh, I could see Harry Bidacker taking notes right then. There were going to be a couple of paras added to my dossier in the morning. And you never get demerits for having a girl like Sarah call you 'darling'. This was integration on an international scale. With this kind of experience behind me, I might one day be safe enough to turn loose in Istanbul where there were so many Russian spies.

And I'd done most of the organization for this party; Harry knew that, too.

He was in a very warm mood. Something had happened in Holland about the Free Trade Area which was a little unnerving, and he'd flown north again wondering whether maybe the firm's policy wasn't a little in advance of the times. Then he had got out of the plane in Scottish sunshine and it had stayed all day and the hotel was warm enough and now here was what looked a great chunk of local Enterprise all drinking the company's gin.

'Well,' Harry said. 'There's no doubt about the young folks knowing each other.'

Sarah smiled at him, moving towards me. Harry took James Baillie's arm and they went off towards the man who would probably be the next Lord Provost, who had brought his lady. She, poor soul, looked both as though she didn't know why she was there, or why she had married her husband. No one had told her about the Peacock Room and she was wearing purple, a lot of it.

Sarah and I stood facing each other and I had nothing to say to her. It was made worse by the fact for the first time completely I was the only reason for her being in the place where she found herself. She was asking me to notice that she had made a special effort to dress up for this party and all I could think of was that I didn't like the result.

'Daddy didn't bully me into coming today, Ned.'

'I . . . didn't think he had.'

'You can stare in a way that really isn't pleasant.'

'Sorry.'

I looked down at the carpet. Across the room that carpet took off and climbed up and wrapped itself around a large frightened woman who still looked human. Sarah didn't.

'All right,' Sarah said bitterly. 'I'm an actress. My whole life is designed for entrances.'

'You didn't need to say that.'

'Oh, for God's sake get me a gin!'

'All right.'

I didn't even have to move. Waiters would always notice Sarah and, for all my height, tend to pass me up for the man with moustaches. Sarah got her drink and I took another.

'You've done pretty well with your collection,' she said, looking around.

I saw Sarah's eyes stop on that mother figure who was now looking a little like a Victorian painting of waiting for Vesuvius to erupt again. Something in me curled up, certain that Sarah would laugh, that she would use what she saw. When she didn't say a word I felt a silly kind of relief. I wanted to put out my hand to touch her, but, still standing there, Sarah had none the less moved off out of reach.

That was when Gracie came in, spotted me, and moved over. There was no sign of Joe. Gracie was wearing silver lamé, a very tight dress, tight all over, with long pointed shoes. Her blonde hair glittered, and an hour at her mirror had slashed ten years off her age.

I'm prejudiced, of course, but to my mind only in America do you find such a large percentage of Gracies, middle-class women who do their own housework and look after the kids, but who can still at thirty-five wriggle themselves down into a dress like that silver lamé, reaching out for a cigarette with hands from a soap powder ad, long pointed nails lacquered.

Gracie and Sarah looked at each other. They each smiled and heard the other's name.

'Where's Joe?'

Gracie's smile stayed social.

'Where do you think? One of Joe's special valves got asthma at the last minute. If it stops breathing there will be some horrible tubular complications all over the works. Joe is right down there in greasy overalls. The most I could get him to do was drive me to the railway station. I just sat beside him swearing all the way and all he said was, "Honey, you know you understand." Sometimes I think it would have been better to have married a Frenchman and learned how to be social to your husband's new mistress at a formal dinner. Excuse me, Miss Baillie, but I'm hopping mad. Get me a drink, Ned!'

I had to move away to do this and when I came back Sarah and Gracie were talking and still smiling. Gracie took her drink, finished it, and held out her glass.

'I'm not driving home,' she said. 'And I propose entering our dear little bungalow singing the hep numbers of my lost youth. Which is Harry Bidacker?'

I told her and Gracie stared across the room.

'His wife,' she said, 'will be president of a Ladies' Literary Luncheon Club. He looks happy. Is everything going all right?'

'Yes, so far.'

'It's a pity our knight declined. I could have told you he was going to. Lady Strathlaird didn't look at all the cocktail party type to me. Ned's a wonderful organizer, Miss Baillie, but our aristocrat got away. Unfortunate. None of these men look capable of noticing a gal's clothes. And you and I have worked hard, haven't we?'

Sarah laughed, as though she meant it. Gracie was looking at the black dress.

'May I call you Sarah? I was just thinking that the chain store adaptation of your model would lose the whole point, wouldn't it? Does your pappy own a lot of Edinburgh?'

'Just bits here and there,' Sarah said.

'I've got a feeling they're the right bits. Have you ever been in America, Sarah?'

'No.'

'I think you'd find it a lovely experience. But never consider marrying one of our men. They make the best husbands in the world. And who wants that?'

I'd had a lot to do with a man in striped pants while making arrangements, and I saw him now, by a gold and white door, giving me a sign. My moving off just then didn't matter the least little bit. I don't think either Sarah or Gracie noticed it, they were intent on the kind of preliminary skirmishing which can lead to a lasting relation between two women, the kind of relation that, for reasons of their own, they may even maintain in the face of a natural antipathy.

'Excuse me, sir,' said striped pants, 'there's a gentleman downstairs. . . .'

For an American there is something extraordinarily satisfying in meeting for the first time in a foreign land an inhabitant who fits in with your preconceived ideas. Britain, for all they may deny it in some places over here, is still divided into the three groups of the Royal Proclamation, the nobility, the gentry, and the commonalty. The man who got up from a sofa to meet me was right outside the commonalty, which had been my only contact up to now. He was in his fifties somewhere, lean, grey-haired, moulded suit resisting bagginess, with a strong hint of starch in collar and cuffs. You could see he'd been a soldier and at least a colonel. He looked at me with a kind of tolerance that suggested something recently acquired, perhaps under the threat of another Socialist government. He might have been in training to get over a natural suspicion for large sections of the human race.

'This is a bit odd,' he said. Then he smiled.

We can imitate this kind of thing in shirt ads in America, but we never really get near it. I could see why Gracie hadn't wanted to use him to promote Harry Bidacker, and I had a moment when I felt like telling him that he couldn't come upstairs with me, that he'd had his chance and turned it down in writing.

'Had to come into Edinburgh today,' he said. 'You know, the whole way I kept thinking we can be damn' stuffy. Never heard of this man Bidacker, of course. Why the hell should I?'

'No reason, Sir Roger.'

'That's what me wife said. But I decided I didn't like it. Came along to say so. Not to crash your party, if that's what you're thinking.'

Every now and then you meet the man who can fix you with an eye which makes honesty not just policy but a kind of moral necessity. I told Sir Roger that Gracie hadn't wanted to invite him. He got that at once.

'Nice gel,' he said.

'Will you come up?' I asked.

'What you got up there? Pack of town worthies?'

'Just about.'

'Well, I'm used to them.'

Suddenly he began to laugh. I had the impression that it was a considerable time since he had surrendered to an impulse in quite this manner. I was also increasingly certain that he had been helped along in his decision by a late and by no means unalcoholic lunch. It seemed more than possible that the idea of joining us had occurred to him well on in that meal, and not, as he said, driving to town.

Gracie's welcome to Sir Roger Strathlaird lacked decent restraint, but he liked it. There were two other men with the girls by that time but it was as though they were lifted up and put neatly to one side. I didn't make the mistake of becoming a third, and went about my business of being a semi-host, which in the course of five minutes brought me up to a figure standing against drapes, the woman in purple. She was holding a glass of tomato juice in one hand and a canapé in the other, and had been quite alone. To defend herself against me she popped the canapé in her mouth and I had to wait.

But my old flair with people's mums wasn't rusty. Soon I heard that her eldest was nearly as tall as me, not quite, but nearly. He had, she said, been sent to Harrow, and this was announced in a tone of loss, as though the step taken had a kind of grim finality about it. Harrow might have been the centre of Africa, remote, infinitely strange . . . England.

It was her husband's doing, sending the boys away, the direct result of a natural Scots pessimism, the feeling that business acumen is rarely inherited and one might as well turn one's progeny into gentlemen. But to the mother the step remained incomprehensible, part of the accelerating pattern of success which left her in a kind of limbo. I suspected she had been warned to prepare for the role of Lady Provost, and now saw her life darkening into a succession of intimidating occasions and weird rituals.

'You know, dear,' she told me, 'I'm not good with a lot of people. It's not a thing I've been used to.'

I tried to change the tomato juice for a sherry, but she wouldn't have it; sherry made her dizzy. There was no escape for her that way, she would always have to be completely responsible through the coming ordeals, keeping alert for Tom's sake. And at the end they would knight Tom, and for the rest of her life she would be officially a lady.

'How about a sandwich?' I said.

'I could do with a sandwich. I must say I didn't know you had any.'

I found some with salmon in them and put the plate on a radiator near us. I was thinking of my dream of the static background, of home that didn't change, where you kept the old frame house and didn't go in for glass walls. This woman would have liked a rocker on the porch, and life mellowing, without having to move too much, or stand in rooms with purple carpets.

We began to talk about the people around us and she forced a kind of sprightly interest.

'I just can't get used to these fashions. Tell me, do men like these kind of clothes on girls?'

'We don't come into it at all.'

'Well, I'm sure I've always tried to dress to please my husband. But some of these things today. There's that girl over there. Why, it looks almost like another skin.'

It was Gracie, and it did, too. A skin you wouldn't try to sit down in.

'And that black!' said the mother of Harrovians.

Sarah had turned and for a moment looked at us.

'Who would she be?'

'Baillie is the name.'

'Not . . . Mr. Baillie's daughter?'

'That's right.'

'Good gracious!'

There was real surprise behind that exclamation, and something else. I turned to look at a broad, plain face which for a moment registered an almost intent curiosity, as though the mention of Mr. Baillie's daughter rang a lot of bells somewhere.

My own curiosity was pretty sharp then, too, and I made the mistake of letting it be seen. As soon as I was established as a friend of Sarah's, what had been an increasingly cosy interlude suddenly became fraught with tensions again. I was something to be got away from as quickly as possible, and my lady in purple said her husband had given her a sign, which was odd since he had his back turned. She went off, boldly, into the crowd.

Was the sharp interest because Sarah was an actress? No, that wasn't good enough, not nearly.

I stood alone for a time watching the final stages in the inevitable converging of Harry Bidacker and Sir Roger. It was like squinting through a microscope at a mating of cells, the two nuclei knew what they were about and steered a deliberate, controlled course, but the movement of the surrounding protoplasm suggested a state of extreme excitement. Even Gracie was nervous about what had to come and was a little shrill.

By the time I got over the two men were talking and Sir Roger had the initiative. He never let it go. It was a triumph of breeding over enterprise. I don't know how many whiskies Sir Roger had taken by that time, but he was at once outrageous with bland good humour.

'My dear man, I've lived long enough to see assorted British Governments pass through some phases of complete lunacy. And the present oil lunacy is the worst of the lot!'

Sir Roger even took time here to smile around at his audience. It was like a signal that we were not to be put out of temper and even Harry reacted. He managed a kind of smile, but no word before the bugles sounded for the next charge.

'If you want to know the truth, we're being sold lock stock and barrel to your companies. Mind you, you've given us a delightful party, but I'm afraid the mention of oil still makes me see red. It's all right for you chaps, you've got the stuff in your country, but for us every new diesel train that's put on the rails means us going down on our knees again to some Arab brigand who's out to take us for a ride and lovin' it. In my

76

own house I have to listen to the blasted bleeps of a new oil thing they're trying out near me. It's perfectly hellish. You know, the only thing that cheers me is the thought of the day of reckoning. I'd like to live to see it. But I'm a fossil already, it won't be in my time.'

Sir Roger then looked directly at me.

'It'll be in yours,' he said.

No one asked him what he meant. We just waited. It came.

'Atomic power, that's what's ahead for you chaps. I'll bet that's the spectre at the board meeting! Thirty years will see it. Texas could be a derelict area. And the Middle East left to sandstorms. Don't take a pension from your company, young man, take a lump sum. You don't get a pension out of a bankrupt business.'

Someone gave Sir Roger a glass of whisky. His smile became almost benign. He sent it out amongst us.

'I'm backin' Rolls-Royce. First atomic car, you know. Think of the oil shares that day, eh? Russian moon rockets aren't in it. Monster panics, what?'

Sir Roger took a long drink and then lifted his glass so that we could see the amber liquid only faintly thinned by water.

'This'll be here,' he said, almost sweetly. 'Actually I have a lot of shares in whisky. Thing I always tell chaps to buy. Never been wrong yet. Got any whisky shares, Mr. Bidacker?'

'No,' Harry said, and that was all he did say.

Seven

SOME girls are doomed to go through the rest of their lives looking as though they had been Head of School and Captain of the Hockey Team. Eileen Baillie was both these things when I met her, and already she had the clear stamp of her future on her; she was big, and made of every movement an excess, she had too much of almost everything, leg, teeth, hair and muscle. She looked at me at once with the sharpest suspicion because I was a friend of her sister's.

I know there is a lot that can be said against the way girls are brought up in the States; that they rush at being women too soon, start dating at fourteen and by seventeen look odd with their faces washed. The fact remains, however, that they stay female. A lot of British girls at fee-paying schools seem to have all the natural consciousness of sex pounded out of them and they can never get back into that track again.

Eileen looked as though she could see no point in this lingering at the edge of a Princes Street pavement. They were going to have coffee, Sarah said, and would I like to join them?

I could see why Sarah issued the invitation. She had been, for some reason, alone with her sister for quite some time and just couldn't bear it any longer. I offered a kind of break in the enduring negative of their relation. To have declined and gone about my business would have been to show a lack of common charity.

We went into one of the bun shops, up in an elevator to a coffee lounge which was packed with middle-aged women in tables of four, eating cakes with highly coloured icing. You could count the men on the fingers of one hand, though I knew they were drinking coffee, too, during business hours, in rooms set aside for them.

There was a nice table for us in the window; a foursome had just risen, and we nipped in with a little triumphant scurrying. Eileen then sat back and looked at me.

I'll say that for them, they're not shy. I was being ticked off against some standard for males and getting a minus mark on every count. Being very young, Eileen had learned no kind of generosity, and it didn't take her long to decide that this was an experience to be got through with the minimum of politeness.

She decided, for one thing, not to talk. This was probably pretty sound, because without doubt there would have been very little chance of establishing any point of contact, but there was always the weather and the imminence of spring, a subject on which I embarked. Eileen went on looking at me, eating a cream puff which she certainly didn't need.

At sixteen one isn't human, but sometimes there are glimmerings of what is to come. You can look at the chrysalis and imagine the folded wings. With Eileen I could only see a steady and solid progress through an uncomplicated world of black and white. She looked calmly at an existence which was pre-ordained, and chewed. If there was any excitement in store for her she would beat it flat with a trained composure.

I asked her if she was playing golf a lot and she considered me an even greater fool for not knowing that this was something which came later in life. Sarah didn't help, either; she was just relaxing into this respite, wanting her coffee.

Eileen looked very much like her mother; she had the same wrists and hands, but much more money was being spent on the girl than had been her mother's portion, with the result that Eileen's voice, though loud, was dull with a basic

79

disinterest in freaks outside an expensive pattern. Sarah and I were both utterly outside it, as far in our different ways, to be endured rather than tolerated.

It went on for a long time, the ritual deliberate, and when we were out in the street again it was noon, and I was angry enough to suggest to Sarah that now the pubs were open we go somewhere and have a drink. At once she agreed and told Eileen what she had to know about their mother's lunch, dismissing her sister with the assured competence of someone who has learned that the way to get out of the path of a steam-roller is to step lightly to one side.

Eileen went off with about as bad a grace as could be imagined, carrying two dangling parcels towards a bus stop. Sarah smiled at me.

'I'd have invested the money at six per cent,' she said, and then began to laugh.

We sat on stools up at the bar.

'I'm grateful to you, Ned. And I'm going to buy you a drink.'

'You owe it. How long do the holidays go on for?'

'Three weeks. It lets me out more.'

'So that you could have dinner with me some night?'

'Make it supper and a theatre. I want to go and see the latest at the local Rep. Will you take me?'

'I will.'

'Ned, dear, you can relax now. Don't go on looking unnerved.'

'I was thinking about being a parent.'

She put her hand over mine.

'You shouldn't try to face these things until you come to them. And I expect one isn't really as troubled as you'd imagine. It's something you've done and you try to make the best of it. You have to, otherwise life wouldn't be bearable. And we mustn't forget that to my mum and pa, Eileen is the family pride and joy. She never does anything they can't foresee. I'm the stinker there, I won't settle. That seems to be a parent's greatest lust, to settle their little ones, early and firmly. Somebody else's Johnny can experiment so that the world doesn't get too dull, but dear God, not mine! I'm quite sure that's the secret prayer. I daresay I'd pray it myself.'

I looked at her. Sarah was as pretty as I'd seen her, eyes alive, nothing else taking her attention. She seemed pleased to be with me. She began to gossip, easily and comfortably, about the people I now knew too. Angus was mysteriously busy in Glasgow and he and Edna had somehow made it up, and she was back playing in the Galt under the director who had trained in variety.

'I knew the gesture didn't mean much,' Sarah said. 'Edna just couldn't resist the opportunity.'

'It could be because she has to eat!'

Sarah smiled.

'That was meant as one between the eyes for little Nell, wasn't it? Darling, listen to me. What do you think I was doing when I was south in Rep and in London? Living off my people and playing at acting? Oh, no. I didn't have a penny from home for the whole time, nor a dress, nor a nice cashmere twin-set, nor a food parcel. The whole time, Ned. The kind of money that Edna has from her Rep would have been riches. I kept my figure by not eating lunches I couldn't afford. And very often no supper, either. I'm telling you this because I want you to know that while I was doing the thing I did it properly. As I would do it again. But not in Edinburgh. Not here in the land of milk and honey and well-heeled papas. There's nothing else to do here but take everything with both hands.'

She looked at her glass.

'Sorry, Ned, I didn't quite mean that. I meant that I'm Papa's daughter now. You do your duty and you get the little black dress. Aren't there all kinds of ways of being a whore?'

'Oh, shut up!'

'You're sensitive. I apologize again. Ned, I have the feeling sometimes that you're waiting around for me. That I could turn a corner anywhere and find you. With a sort of patience. And it's not the sort of patience of someone who's got

everything planned and wants to fit me into the plan somewhere. I don't feel that with you. It may be why I run away.
Do you know what I'm talking about?'

'Yes.'

'And is it true? You haven't got any plans? Nothing
specific? You don't have a role in your life waiting for me?'

'I haven't plotted it out, if that's what you mean.'

'Thanks. It's so nice not to be plotted out. Ned, I was once
in love with a man who looked very like you.'

'I know.'

Her eyes widened.

'Oh. So it's the village again? The dear little village. Just
give me a minute, I'll get it. Yes! Edna told you that night you
came into the Café Royal and I was having dinner with Ralph.
Is that it? But of course. Ned, have you thought about it at all,
that you looked like someone I was in love with?'

'Sometimes.'

'It explained a lot, didn't it? A girl kisses you in a car and you
think opportunity has knocked again. But it's only because
you looked like somebody else and the girl had taken too
many gins.'

'That's right.'

'It's not right. I'm not in love with my man down in London
any more. I can look back at what I thought we felt and see two
fools, me and him. I didn't even bring my suffering home with
me.'

'Sarah, I'm sorry about Harry Bidacker's party.'

'You mean the way you looked at me? As though you would
have dissociated yourself from me in a Paris boulevard.'

'I've said I'm sorry!'

'It was really rather a nice party. Created by Ned. Did you
get a lot of credit for it?'

'Not as much as I'd hoped.'

'You mean your Harry was a little upset by Sir Roger?'

'I mean he flew to Mexico with indigestion.'

'And that can have repercussions?'

'It might, I suppose.'

'It's odd, Ned, how we go about things the same way. You were trying so hard. You hitch on charm like a pair of false whiskers. Are you really very ambitious?'

'I didn't used to think so. Maybe I've changed. Perhaps I am.'

'You are. It's why we should be pals. And you should let me buy my share of the drinks. What happened to Gracie? I didn't see her as we were leaving.'

'She was probably away getting ready to be driven home in Sir Roger's Bentley. Anyway that's what happened.'

Sarah laughed.

'She's amusing.'

'I'm glad you liked her, Sarah.'

'I didn't say I liked her. I said she was amusing. I found her completely organized, all her life. It's quite frightening. She carries her own world around with her ready to unpack it out of a suitcase anywhere. In that way you and she are alike, both the travellers. It's not easy for people who are bound to their villages to like the travellers. You put us in perspective, for one thing, and our world diminishes. You're here today but tomorrow you may be . . . Where may you be, Ned?'

'Palembang, in Sumatra, in six months.'

'You know?' she asked sharply.

'Not exactly. I just had a hint from Harry. It was something on the cards and I have the feeling that now he may accelerate it.'

'Accelerate it!' Sarah laughed.

She suddenly leaned across the bar and said to the man in the white jacket.

'Any tips today, Mac?'

'Well, Miss, some fancy Enterprise.'

'I'll make a note of it. Another two Martinis please.'

Sarah opened her bag and found a bill. She also made a note of the horse.

'Nice man. His tips often come up. So you may be packing your suitcase, Ned? And two days later you'll unpack again in

Palembang and there's a new world waiting. What does it really feel like?'

'A bit queer at first.'

'But you soon settle in, don't you? You have your introductions and those king-sized olives reach there, too. And you have real American evenings.'

'I think you're getting the wrong picture. It's not always going to be a suitcase for me. I want to strike roots as much as anyone.'

Sarah picked up the green olive on its toothpick and moved it up and down in the glass.

'Where would you like to strike roots, Ned?'

'Does that matter?'

For a minute she said nothing, and she didn't look up.

'It would matter to me. I'm easily scared. I like the sights and smells I'm used to. And the faces, too. I always make my village as small as possible. In Rep and in London I was the one who never wanted to change our pub. Or the place we ate. Silly, isn't it? But that's why Edinburgh is so irresistible. It's the perfect village. Nothing ever happens that you can't foresee. Even in the war no one dropped a bomb on it. Oh, they started a Festival afterwards, but we swallowed that in one gulp. It doesn't offer any surprises any more. Edinburgh has sieved down world culture to a fine digestible pulp. And I'm afraid I very much like it that way.'

'Have you been thinking about marrying your Ralph?'

'No, that wasn't a temptation. He would make me do everything I didn't want to for my own good, like watching rugger and playing golf and going down to Gullane for the week-ends. And we'd have four children on the American plan, but not to beat the Russians, just to keep the money in the family.'

She looked at me and smiled.

'There's also that little feeling in the pit of your stomach,' she said. 'I don't get it with Ralph. And it isn't only that he makes me eat too much.'

'Talking of that feeling, I have it now.'

Sarah nodded.

'I know, sweetie. Isn't it hell for both of us?'

We had seats in the third row of the stalls. The Rep was a converted picture house, and what had once been the cheapest seats were now the dearest ones. That was about the only change which had been made, except for heavy curtains and the two faces of drama in papier-mâché over the proscenium. The stage was too wide and very shallow, which almost gave an effect of 3-D stereophonic to the sets, and you had the feeling sometimes that it would help the proportions of things if the actors and actresses would lie down crossways.

However, no one took time to lie down in this play. It was an action drama converted from a Waverley novel, full of clash and costumes and actresses working like hell to be human when the original author hadn't thought of them that way at all.

I should point out here that all us travellers have a kind of prejudice against the theatre. We have to spend most of our lives without its conventions and find the discipline of acceptance a little hard to come by. For instance, I was very conscious throughout this play of those two faces of drama looking down at me. One of them positively stared, as though checking up on the reactions of the most expensive part of the audience.

I doubt very much if I could have stood up to the institution of marriage in Sir Walter Scott's day. His women of gentle breeding, on stage or in print, make one want to whimper for a little sin.

'Is there a bar?' I asked Sarah after the first act.

'No, sweetie, soft drinks. Or ice cream.'

The lights were harsh while we waited, and all around the audience stared at us, as though surprised to find people of our years up where it cost real money. A lot of boxes of chocolates came out and everyone thought the actors just did it beautifully. I became conscious of Sarah looking at me.

'You're restive, Ned.'

'It's a long interval. And I got long legs.'

'You don't like the play?'

'Well . . . no.'

'I agree, it's lousy. But there are two good performances. That's not enough to interest you?'

'Not really, no. But I'm not blaming the actors, Sarah. It's the man who did the conversion job I'd go after. I've been in Scotland for a year and I'm a little tired of your two literary gods.'

'Meaning Burns and Scott? Haven't you forgotten Stevenson?'

'Sorry, three gods. Do they do conversion jobs on Stevenson, too?'

'They do,' Sarah said coldly.

The lights went out and the curtain went up on the stage. The heroine was alone, she didn't like being alone, she was frightened.

No play has ever seemed longer to me. At the start of the third act I realized the pubs had already shut and there was no place in Edinburgh where you could get a drink unless you went to a hotel and had a sandwich, and I didn't want a sandwich. I became more and more conscious that I was behaving extremely badly, even by a tightly held silence, and that Sarah had removed herself, shutting me out.

She was quite right, but I couldn't really help it, I just felt anti, like a child possessed of the devil during a particularly elongated sermon.

On the way out, while we waited for the crowd to thin along the gangways, Sarah stood with her chin lifted, looking beautiful. Her profile was defined and clear, with a kind of perfection that you sometimes missed when you saw her full face. Then you had to have the interest added, or laughter, but always, turned away from you, looking at someone else, she was lovely.

It was one of those moments when you could stand quite still at the edge of something, knowing you were committed, but free, able to assess, able to be a little frightened for yourself and for one other.

She turned and looked at me.

'Coming?'

'Sure.'

People were still loitering in the lobby, standing about under studio portraits of the company. You recognized your friends and called out to them. There was a friendly feeling about it, the village feeling, the director should have been there shaking hands.

'How are you Sarah?' I heard a voice say. 'We rather thought we might see you on this stage one of these evenings.'

Sarah laughed.

'No one has asked me yet.'

She was facing a woman a head taller than she was, in the fifties somewhere, in black, and almost excessively groomed for these surroundings, with a little hat that might have been meant for a cocktail party. There was white hair under it with a blue tint, and pearls at the neck and in her ears. My guess was that they were real pearls; they had the depth and warmth.

I was introduced to a Mrs. Harris who looked at me with quick, sharp interest and then switched it off. She talked almost exclusively to Sarah in a voice just edged with conscious refinement, and all the time I had the feeling that Sarah was surprised at being singled out in this way, that she didn't know the woman well. The talk was about Papa Baillie and his plan to go in for civil politics. Mrs. Harris approved, she was most vehement in her approval, it was a wonderful thing.

We were offered a lift, but got out of that, and on the pavement I found I was still curious.

'What is she in Edinburgh?' I asked.

'Oh, she killed her husband.'

'Poison or a revolver?'

'Politics,' Sarah said.

We got in my car, slammed the doors, and lit cigarettes.

'How do you kill a husband by politics, Sarah?'

'Well, first you snatch a slightly tired jam king from his factory in the middle of Angus berry-fields. You bring him to a house in Edinburgh and then set yourself up as a hostess. You prod your husband into local government and push him on in it by entertaining everyone who matters. You never notice he's getting more and more tired; you have your eye on those highest civic honours and the automatic title that comes with them. You want to be a Lady. Then your husband just dies.'

'And where does that leave Mrs. Harris?'

'Hungry,' Sarah said.

I drove off. The night was mild enough to keep the window down, one of those sudden gentle spells at the end of winter which seem to promise a warmth later that never quite happens in Scotland. There were stars and a new moon and my instinct was to drive Sarah home by the Braid Hills, to park up there with the lights of the city beneath us. My car was the only real privacy we had together, almost big enough to be a moving living-room, but there was a kind of bar against my taking this initiative. I wasn't making any claims; Sarah had to give a sign, and just now I was certain she wasn't going to.

We stuck to the main bus route, through the lights. I drove her carefully to her house and into the drive and up to that portico which sent out no welcome signs. At once Sarah got out of the car and came around to my door, opening it.

'Good night, sweetie. I hate to think of you driving that long dull road.'

She kissed me and shut my door. I slipped into gear and drove out the other gate and I remembered suddenly that first day with Sarah, standing at the Forth Bridge, and wondering where I might be going with this girl. I still didn't know.

Eight

THE letter from my mother was a shock. It began with a long account of the state of my father's sinuses, went on to the new minister who had decided to dress the choir in gowns and make them march up in procession, something unheard of in Abilene with the Baptists. She then sprang her surprise.

You know, Ned, dear, I've always wanted to see you in one of the places where you work and ever since I knew you were going to Scotland I've just hugged a little scheme to myself. Well, you remember I wrote you about those shares I bought in Amalgamated Utilities and your father said this was what came of having women sit around drinking coffee in a stockbroker's office instead of in somebody's living-room? They went up and up and up. What your father forgets is that we are an organized unit of women investors, and that we have good advice and the benefit of nation wide market research. But Amalgamated was really a hunch. I mean, it was well recommended but it wasn't starred. I just plunged. Well, I sold out last week and I've made seventeen hundred dollars. You should have seen your father's face!

I'm not reinvesting, I'm selling some more shares and bringing Louise to Europe this summer. I thought about bringing Sam, too, but he's got his College Boards coming up again and though I know he must get through *this* time . . . he's been working so hard, poor boy . . . I just thought that after he hears it might be as well if he went off to camp. Louise and I are not flying, we're sailing on the *Queen Elizabeth* on July 19th, and though it may seem a bit funny, we decided to go on to Italy first and do Scotland last, just in time for the first of the Edinburgh Festival. What you can do for us is to get three seats for a lot of things, but I would list primarily music, drama and the ballet. We've got the brochure over here and there seems to be a lot of wonderful things!

And there's another thing, Ned, and this is really terribly important. As you know, your great-grandfather on my side of the family was a MacDonald from a little farm on an island called Islay somewhere out in the Atlantic. He left for America in 1847 and I'm told that there will certainly be records of where he lived on the island. Well, I'm not coming to Scotland without making a little pilgrimage. Maybe the house he lived in doesn't exist any more, but there will be something, some stones in the heather, just something that will have meaning to us as a family. It would be a wonderful thing if you could manage to go out there and do a little research before we arrive because we'll only manage two weeks in Scotland and one of them will be at the Festival. I looked it up on the map and it doesn't seem any distance at all. I'm counting on you to do this for us Ned, and I'm sure you will, for you've always been the reliable one. . . .

That was my rating at home, A for reliability, and somewhere about C minus as an object of interest. There is something a little dull about the type who doesn't have to worry over his College Boards, possibly because he wasn't given a car of his own at sixteen during his junior year in High School. Sam, of course, like Eileen Baillie, was a later product in the parental success story. He went with the patio and the glass walls.

I sat there in my small bedroom in Grangemouth, in front of a gas fire which popped occasionally, and wondered whether I was excited at the prospect of showing Scotland to my mother. I think probably right until that moment I had been a loyal enough American boy to shut the door firmly on any objective consideration of the woman who had taken time off to bring me into life. What I was doing now was a little bit indecent. But I did it.

Those two weeks would be devoted to her. That doesn't seem a long time, unless you knew my mother. She has great charm, she is still good-looking, she dresses extremely well, but all other human life, including family, friends and casual contacts, has to be in orbit around her. The centre is where she is.

In the fall I might be in Palembang. I knew then just how much I wanted this summer in Scotland, wanted it whole, to allow the shape it was going to take to grow naturally, without any interruptions.

Louise was nineteen. She was a sophomore at college in Dallas, and she wrote me every time she got a new boy friend, which was nine letters in four years. She'd probably meet the tenth boy on board the '*Lizzie*', and the chances were that he would deviate from his arranged schedules and stay with her, so that three seats to everything would turn out to be one short all the way, and I might as well get four now.

My family were already looming on the horizon, and the great charm of a solitary life was suddenly forced on my attention, not quite in the way that Angus would have had me notice it, but still real for all that. I was already a kind of agency for relations and I knew that I'd better get out to that island soon and start looking for traces of MacDonalds amongst the moss-covered rocks. My mother would write now every ten days to find out what I'd done about that and about seats. When I sent her my list of cultural reservations she'd cancel three items and want replacements.

I got up and went around to Gracie's. Joe was down at the works and the kids were at a party. At first because of the quiet I thought no one was at home, and then Gracie came to the door and shouted through it:

'Just turn the handle. I can't because I'm drying nail varnish.'

We sat in the kitchen and drank rye on the rocks. Gracie was up on the table in a housecoat which was bright red and suited her because she had remembered her lipstick. She swung her legs, back and forth, good legs.

'There's something wrong with Junior. Mum always knows. Give.'

I told her. She said, 'Oh, isn't that awful!'

But I didn't have the whole of her attention, there was something else, very large and very looming. She looked at me in speculation, rating a risk.

'Ned, dear, I'm facing that great challenge that comes into the life of every personable woman at thirty-five.'

'Another man?'

'Aren't you cunning? Go on, guess.'

'Sir Roger?'

'You'd make a horrible husband. He's asked me to lunch.'

'It's not a terrible risk, Gracie.'

'It is to me. I'd got to the stage where I thought that nothing like this would ever happen again.'

'Does Joe know?'

'Of course he doesn't know. There'd be no challenge if he did. Sir Roger phoned one morning. I'm pretty sure it was from his estate office. He said he had to be in Stirling on business and he wondered if we might have a spot of lunch. In that glossy hotel. I think Stirling is out of his county.'

'What did you say?'

'I said I often went to Stirling to shop and I'd love to. But ever since remorse has gnawed at me. Ned, I'm the mother of three little ones, and here I am on the brink of what every American woman thinks Europe is like.'

'It'll be something to remember out in Borneo.'

'You don't get the point. That man does something to me. It's a kind of excitement, and I don't think it's healthy. And it's all so easy. I just get Mrs. Carswell in for the kids and go off to shop. Is the downward path always greased up like this?'

'You'll be home by three o'clock, Gracie, and it'll have done you good. You won't have heard any of his stories and he won't have heard any of yours. That's the tonic of all new contacts.'

'You're wise beyond your expeience. It'll get you into an awful lot of trouble one of these days. How's Sarah?'

'Being a dutiful daughter most of the time. And when she's not doing that, she's thinking about a part in some play.'

'Which burns you up a little?'

'Quite a lot, as a matter of fact.'

92

'Ned, I'm no use for your problem and you're no use for mine. We might as well finish the bottle.'

I didn't see Sarah for a week, and during that time she was in Glasgow. She phoned me up when she came back and asked me to meet her in the upstairs of the Café Royal. She was there when I arrived, seated on one of the red leather chairs, and I saw her as I came up the stairs.

She was wearing green again, a colour she seemed to like, the dress with sleeves so tight they made her arms seem a little thin. She already had a drink.

'Hullo, sweetie, I brought you in all that way?'

'I don't have to keep my eyes open, Sarah, the car knows the road. You look all right.'

She smiled.

'Thanks.'

'In fact you look more than that. Something very nice has happened to you.'

'Yes. Ned, have you ever heard of an American called Maxwell Anderson? And a play called *Mary of Scotland*?'

'I have. And I read it at college.'

'We're going to do it at the Festival.'

'You're . . . ? Who?'

'Angus. Oh, we're not official. But this is one of Angus's projects. His first serious one, really. And he's been terribly lucky. One of the halls here that is usually booked up from one year to another for Fringe productions has suddenly fallen empty. Angus nipped in and got it before he knew what he was going to use it for. Then he looked about for his play. I think he's been very shrewd. There are more Americans coming than ever this year, and even a revival by one of their own countrymen is going to be something that they will all want to see. And the hall is central. The Fringe has become almost as important as the official Festival. All kinds of things have happened from it.'

'Sarah, what are you thinking?'

She put out her hand and touched mine.

93

'I don't really know. All I can say is that the moment I heard about this I could feel the excitement bottling up in me. And that was before I even knew what was in Angus's mind, what his full plans were.'

'When you heard them you learned about the casting, is that it?'

She nodded.

'Yes. I'm to play Mary of Scotland.'

I just looked at her. That seemed to make her nervous; her head jerked away, up towards the bar, so that I saw her profile again. But tonight she was as beautiful when she looked at me. After a moment I asked my question.

'And who is Queen Elizabeth?'

Sarah's eyes met mine.

'Don't laugh. Edna.'

I didn't laugh. I could just see it. I'd felt Angus's power, his flair for what he did best; you could even call it more than flair. Sarah and Edna, the antagonists in the play. What a lot they were both going to have to help them.

'I know Mary was six feet tall and a redhead,' Sarah said. 'But it doesn't matter. Not for the image people have of her in their minds.'

She was right, it didn't matter.

'Sarah, I'm trying to remember the play. I can't very well. But isn't it the conventional angle, Mary the innocent victim, Elizabeth the politician?'

'In a way, yes. But what do you mean, Ned? From your experience of Scots women do you doubt the innocence?'

She was laughing but it wasn't in her eyes.

'Are you doing this for the whole three weeks?' I asked.

'Yes. Angus is going to stage it wonderfully; he's got the money. He's starting with a splash. He's got a top designer for the sets. And the dresses for Edna and me are going to be done in Dublin, by that Irish woman whose clothes you can wear ten years later. Can't you see it, Ned? The whole show marvellously dressed and presented. It was the sort of chance I never thought could come to me in Scotland, I never dreamed of it. It's like everything opening out . . . if I can do it. Angus says I can. He says I'll get the feel of the part, that it'll bite into me. Maybe he's right. . . .'

'Of course he's right!'

'Ned, you're not just saying that? You've seen me acting . . . in that Galt thing. I never touched anything, I know that. I haven't done it often, only once or twice. Down south I had a lot of experience but most of it was dead. I mean . . . this mayn't be easy for you to see. I'm not really a good actress in the sense that I can produce a high average. I don't. Most of the time, nearly all of it, I go through the motions and get by with a little more than the minimum. I know that, I'm not trying to fool you or anyone. But it *has* been different. Once in a play I didn't like. It was *The Sacred Flame*. I thought it dated and falsely sentimental, with the wrong feeling all along the way. That was the way I felt about it, and I hadn't a very sympathetic part; I was the nurse. But it happened. It was just real, that's all, night after night for two weeks. Maybe the play is better than I thought, but I hadn't any perspective on it at all after rehearsals, I just cared what I was. And for the time I wasn't anything else. Does this seem a lot of nonsense to you?'

'No, Sarah.'

'Oh, Ned, I have the most terrible feeling that I mustn't let this new thing get away. That I'm going to have to fight, and start fighting now.'

'With the part?'

'Yes. I'm going away somewhere, next month I think, or perhaps in May. We've got someone who'll come for a time to look after Mother. I'll take the play and nothing else.'

'For how long, Sarah?'

'Oh, maybe a couple of weeks. I want to go quite a time before we start rehearsals. So I can build the thing up to a sort of pitch and let it go again. That way you have something to work towards when you've actually come to the business with the other players. I'm lucky to be able to do this, to have the time. None of the others will. But I think I need it much more than they do. Edna will just walk through Elizabeth, it's something she could do after a week.'

'You're trembling, Sarah.'

'Am I? Silly of me.'

'Would you like another drink?'

'No, thanks. You're sweet. You've somehow made it possible for me to tell what I feel like. When I was waiting I thought perhaps I'd been rather a fool to phone off to you like that. Ned . . . you . . .'

'What is it?'

'You . . . you don't butt in. But I'm so glad you're here.'

The lights about there were a bit too bright for me just then.

'If you don't want another drink, Sarah, how about us going? You haven't got a car?'

'No, I came by bus.'

We went out and got into that movable living-room and sat along the front sofa. I fiddled around with the radio and brought in some soft dance music. She didn't ask why we weren't driving off, but leaned her head back and took the cigarette I gave her. A policeman came out of his little box and looked in at us. It had been raining and the pavements glistened and feet coming towards us and going away were noisy.

'Sarah, I'm going away too, sometime soon.'

She sat up.

'You don't mean leaving Scotland?'

'Oh, no. I've got a commission from my mother. She's coming over for the Festival. You'll meet her. I've got to go out and look for ancestors on an island called Islay.'

Sarah sat back again.

'You don't pronounce the *y*,' she said.

'Thanks. That's a good start. Now I'll be able to buy my ticket. Sarah . . . I could go almost any time. I mean I've got holiday time due, I've only got to take it.'

She didn't seem to be listening. It was cold in the car so I switched on the engine and then the heater.

'Damn it, I love you,' I said.

'Please don't, Ned. Please don't say things we . . . we can't live up to.'

'All right. Is it the same old routine to Morningside?'

'Yes, please.'

But she didn't get out when we reached the house. It was funny to sit there in front of that mass of unlit black stone, knowing that somewhere inside, unless she had the TV on full, Mrs. Baillie must have heard a car draw up.

'Ned, I've been thinking about what you said. I was a bit startled. I mean I thought I had to be alone, naturally. The idea of anyone else . . . But I see that I'd like it to be with you. I'd like to go to your Islay. I've never been there.'

My heart was thumping. Sarah turned to me, her eyes wide. She wasn't thinking about being Mary of Scotland just then.

'You . . .' she said.

Nine

In April the sun shone and even the road past the coal bings was alive, the green weeds coming through. Beyond the bleak belt I saw horses ploughing on a steep hill. The farmer must have kept them for that field, because there was the sound of a tractor, too, but the horses cut their own sharp furrow, big brutes, with furred feet, and straight above them was the high Scots sky, blue, with small white clouds blowing from the west in little flocks untended.

At one point the road swelled up on to high ground and you could see Edinburgh Castle, perhaps ten miles ahead, the light hard on it, and warm. The Pentland Hills were mountains, with snow on the peaks, though you could climb them from a bus stop in half an hour. When you got to the villas the matched tedium of bay windows and two chimneys was somehow accentuated by daffodils; everybody had them, and grew them in tidy, geometric plots, the same yellow, a long undulation of colour behind the curving road which took the traffic from Glasgow.

Gracie was beside me. She was going into Edinburgh to buy a hat. She said she mustn't miss her chance in this country because she was quite certain that a Scotch hat would last her for the rest of her life.

'All those daffodils remind me,' Gracie said. 'I've got to fix a date for us to go to Cambenden. That's their estate.'

'Gracie, dear, it's egocentric to expect me to be following your thought. I have my own. What the hell is Cambenden?'

'It's Sir Roger's estate. And it's a place of pilgrimage at this time of year because of the daffodils. There are a million or something and three days a week just now the gardens are open and buses come with thousands from Glasgow and Edinburgh and Dundee and Perth. Sir Roger is giving us a private view. One of the days when the gates are shut to the rabble.'

'Count me out,' I said.

Gracie didn't seem to hear.

'There is also the famous Cambenden vine. It is housed in acres of glass-houses and it gives an average yearly yield of seven hundred bunches of black grapes. And if I sound like a guide-book it's because I've been reading one. The mansion is not historic.'

'With all those grapes he shouldn't have to show any family ghost at a dollar a time. Think of it, Gracie, a big bunch will have three or four pounds, at five shillings a pound out of season . . . well, that's a nice little item to forget to tell your tax man about.'

'I see you're interested in the vine, Ned. And I'm sure we'll be allowed to have a look at it. I told Sir Roger that there would be twenty-three of us including the kids and we'd come in our own cars.'

'I take it all this was a result of your lunch?'

She looked at me and smiled.

'That's right. Have you noticed how I've been avoiding being alone with you so you wouldn't have a chance to ask me how that went?'

'How did it go, Gracie?'

'We had a good meal, with no Scots emphasis on carbohydrates. We told a few stories and then Sir Roger became serious about life. He's developed a simple soldier's philosophy and I found it incredibly touching. I can't say at what point exactly I realized I ought to be thinking about Joe again, but that moment came. I put up all the signal flags which said I was a wife and mother. And he sent back a message that he hadn't really meant anything, and we both knew we weren't telling the whole truth. So you see, I might just as well be gadget-minded. In every other respect I'm completely suburban.'

'And where did the daffodils come into it?'

'Well, we had to wind up the occasion. I thought a private view was a terribly graceful way of doing it. You know, bringing all the kids.'

'Making it a kind of mass American thanksgiving for the end of another Scots winter?'

'Don't be unpleasant, Ned. You're coming. I intend to organize this occasion and it isn't going to rain. You'll bring Sarah to Grangemouth and we'll all go in convoy. And this time Joe'll be one of us, I'll see to that.'

'It's the last kind of party you'd ever find Sarah on,' I said.

But here I was very wrong. Sarah wanted to go as soon as she heard about it, and when the day came I stopped grumbling, for Gracie had organized it, and though it wasn't really warm, there was a lemon sun with mist on high ground. The convoy had six cars led by Gracie and Joe in an American Ford and finished off by Sarah and me in the Pontiac. We wound in and out amongst those Scottish hills that looked like mountains and it was comfortable in the cars with the heating on.

Sarah had slipped out of her shoes and had her feet up on the seat, sitting in close against me, which wasn't at all unpleasant. She had that flair, really only given to women of temperament, for making the inauspicious memorable, and I was quite certain that if we married everything would go wrong with the solemn recurring anniversaries, whatever I arranged for these ceremonies dead mutton. Now, because of my reluctance, she meant to enjoy her day.

'Ned, if you lag behind like this we'll lose them.'

'I hate driving on anyone's tail and I hate having someone nosing along behind me.'

'Still, get just a little closer. I don't think it's far now and you never really see the gates to these places. They're usually half-camouflaged.'

'In the hope that the revolution will sweep by and not notice?'

Sarah laughed.

'You know, there's something very appealing about that idea. And you've got to admit that it's a perfect country this for little Shangri-las. You could have a drive that just sneaked on to a main road so that no one would ever notice, made to look like a farm track. But as you got on through the trees it improved and then you came to the house. Facing south, of course. Nothing but hills and the corner of a loch, and your family portraits and old furniture and a walled garden. The house would be Georgian and they have a kind of pinky stone up here that's wonderful with a white trim. Not big, about seven bedrooms.'

'How many servants?'

'Just a couple. Wonderful retainers, you know. Always have huge fires burning when you come back from visiting other hidden houses in the neighbourhood and plain, hot food waiting.'

'Complete escapism.'

'Absolutely. And don't pretend you don't have it in the States. I saw an ad in an American magazine for a house in Vermont, stone-built, atom bomb-proof, hydrogen bomb-resistant.'

'If you wanted that kind of security,' I said loudly, 'why didn't you set out to marry it?'

Sarah moved against me, slightly.

'It's not so easy.'

'With your looks? Are you going to tell me you should have gone to your sister's school?'

'Oh, no, my sister's school wouldn't really have helped at all. It's not easy to become county in Scotland. You can buy the house if you have money, but the baby Austins from the other houses like it probably just go on missing your drive. I wouldn't want to be lonely, I'd like the tight comfort of that small world, of only appearing in public in special roped-off areas. You know everyone inside the ropes and no one outside.

Everyone is everyone else's cousin. The men wear the kilt a lot and the women the same kind of tweeds, cut by a one-eyed tailor in Perth. I've seen it sometimes from a distance and thought it was probably the only way even to begin to feel snug in the second half of the twentieth century. It mayn't last, but it's nice while it does.'

'You'd be bored silly!'

'I wonder? There's a lot to do, you know. All splendidly extrovert and hearty. For instance I would fish.'

She waited until I had finished laughing.

'Why do you think it funny that I would fish?'

'I thought you were all burned up about being Mary of Scotland?'

'If I sneaked into the little world as an outsider I'd be so busy acting all the time that I wouldn't miss the stage. I'd be competing against centuries of training, trying to make myself look like I had it too, when I don't. Absorbing.'

'They're turning off,' I said.

'Yes, and look at the gates. As a tourist you'd just whiz by and never notice.'

The cars had all slowed down, because they had to. The macadam surface ended suddenly, switching to dirt under trees, and ruts with stones strewn around. Sarah sat up and put on her shoes as we heaved about. There wasn't a daffodil in sight, just damp woods that needed thinning, the sun not getting through them, the feel of winter held here.

There wasn't a house in sight, either; it could have been somewhere up in Newfoundland, with the evergreens and little clumps of silver birch. An hour's drive took you to a city, but right then it was difficult to believe.

I missed seeing a pot-hole and we really caught it, the wheel shivering in my hands. The cars up front were weathering heavy seas, too. I saw one side-swiping some overhanging bushes. I could almost hear American curses on the Scots spring air.

The house surprised us; it was just suddenly there, big and looming, turning a solid face to the approaches, with windows high enough up to be designed for defence. As the guide-book had warned us it wasn't an historic house; a Strathlaird with a lot of money must have put it up about a hundred years ago, turrets and all. Dry rot hadn't driven the descendants out yet, but it probably would.

We all got out of the cars in a crescent of nicely raked gravel which began as suddenly as the smooth road surface had ended. Doors slammed and the stillness vibrated to the cries of kids running for the shelter of the rhododendron bushes.

'John-ee,' shrilled a voice. 'Not there, son. Right in behind!'

Just then Sir Roger came down the steps. He was wearing the kilt, a tartan with a lot of green and red in it as well as an improbable yellow. He looked a shade menacing and said at once, loudly, with a kind of trained briskness:

'Well, you've all got here.'

There was more than a suggestion of his bus party manner in this. You felt at once that this really should have been one of the days when just down there where the gravel ended a man would be sitting at a table to collect the visitors' half-crowns.

The kids were streaming back from the bushes, full of immediate plans for the kind of independent action we're all brought up to. They had reckoned without Sir Roger. For one thing they'd never quite heard a voice like his. It was louder than their combined effort, distinct and demanding immediate attention.

'This is a good place to start,' he said. 'Shall we all get together for it?'

In other words, fall in. I noticed one or two of our mothers almost making defensive movements towards their little ones, and there was a good deal of protest, but that was shushed, and in about two minutes we were a flower-viewing unit, with Gracie and Joe up there in a privileged position near the commander and behind them a long straggle of irregulars. One of the kids started to bawl but we moved off none the less.

'I'm taking you through the herbaceous,' Sir Roger shouted. 'Damn all to see now, of course. But it's the shortest way, actually.'

About then a wind got up, a sneak of a wind that had been waiting for this, worming its way through the hills of that sheltered southern-facing position to hit us smack in the middle of the herbaceous. The wind came from Aberdeen that afternoon, and beyond that the North Sea, and beyond that Russia.

I'd left my coat in the car and Sarah, in a lightish two-piece, hadn't brought one. She ignored the wind.

'I'm told,' she said, 'that if you only know the Latin names of three slightly unusual plants, you can get through any Scottish herbaceous garden in high summer with full credits. Do you know any Latin names?'

'Aquilegia,' I said.

'Splendid. Try it later. Isn't this fun?'

'If you want to know, it's even worse than I expected.'

'You shouldn't try to resist discipline,' Sarah said. 'You ought to relax and enjoy it.'

'Where are those daffodils?'

'There.'

She was right; they were ahead, half a hill of them. Maybe Wordsworth wasn't cold; I just looked. I could see the daffodils weren't liking the wind either, far from happy in their Highland surroundings, more like refugees. Those flowers weren't dancing, they were trying to lie down.

'Of course we're really madly sheltered here,' Sir Roger bellowed.

Sarah began to laugh.

Later on we were allowed into the main building, all of us. Into the hall. This had been built by a Strathlaird who thought his own particular kind of democracy was going to last for ever. He had built firmly, with a massive lack of taste that could only inspire awe. The roof went up and up and was finally supported by molasse gargoyles. Facing the front door was the main stair, which looked as though it had been designed for family reunions in a period when questions of precedence could cause bloodshed. Ten Strathlairds could have come down those stairs abreast, with drawn swords.

There was a huge chimney-piece and, where the glowing logs should have been, a paraffin stove sent out a kind of snigger of heat. Near this was a trestle-table, an emergency device clearly, presided over by a frightened-looking and aged female retainer in a lace cap. There was the kind of urn you see in a railway buffet over here, and obviously this feeding drill was something all laid on for occasions like a night with the Women's Rural Institute.

Our kids were hungry. They'd never had fish-paste sandwiches before and didn't think a lot of them. Our mothers, edgy, moved in with a fine show of discipline and practically went in for forced feeding, trying at the same time to appear cheerful.

Amongst us moved Sir Roger and his wife, neither of them eating anything. Lady Strathlaird was the sort of woman who made you suddenly conscious of her husband's age. He could have been anything from forty-five onwards, but his wife placed him, wearing a chatelaine dress in grey wool that only needed its bunch of keys. Her hair was grey, too, and her skin like slightly weathered parchment. She moved, a wraith through the age in which she found herself, not even pretending to be at home in it. It was only when you came close that you noticed her mouth, colourless but firm, and her faded eyes looked like they could get very cold indeed.

Duty brought her to me. You could see she was punctilious about duty.

'You're in oil, too, are you? I'm afraid my husband gets rather cross about it. Personally I've found it very convenient. It saves putting on so many fires.'

She smiled, and might have been inspecting the panelling behind me. Her voice was a grey monotone.

'What did you think of the daffodils?'

'I've never seen anything quite like them, Lady Strathlaird.'

'No, I suppose not. We've been massing them there for

about a hundred years. Actually for myself I prefer the tulips when they come. I find all that yellow a little trying.'

'I can quite see your point, ma'am.'

The little courtesy which came fairly naturally to me made her flick her eyelids up. After a moment she said, as though she had considered it carefully first:

'You should come in summer. Our borders are supposed to be exceptional. Of course we're extraordinarily sheltered here. Not that things are quite as we'd like them. We've only one man outside now. We just manage and no more. Are you enjoying Scotland?'

'Very much indeed.'

'Oh. You don't have a lot of complaints like most Americans?'

'No, ma'am.'

'I must tell my husband that. He says Americans never like anything but America except when they're there. I'm not sure I know what he means, do you?'

'I could have a stab at his meaning, Lady Strathlaird.'

'Could you? Did anyone give you a sandwich?'

'Yes, thank you.'

'Who's that pretty gel over there? Is she American, too?'

'No, that's Miss Baillie from Edinburgh. She's the only one of our party today who isn't American.'

Lady Strathlaird's pale eyes stayed fixed on Sarah.

'Baillie? I don't think we know them. Perhaps Roger might. I believe there are some Baillies in the Borders. But I must speak to her.'

Sarah might have been waiting for that. I think she heard, at any rate she turned.

I don't quite know what I'd been expecting, perhaps a performance that would seem, up against Strathlaird pallor, too lush. But Sarah hit it at once, starting on a muted note which suggested her presence at one of the last Court Presentations, followed by a career which somehow hadn't spoiled the sweet child of the Swiss finishing school. She left the initiative to Lady Strathlaird, a compliment always appreciated by those of advancing years, and almost at once was established as the odd girl out on this weird American picnic.

When Sarah spoke her voice was nearly an octave higher, flattened out into the attenuated whine of breeding. Her laugh was a little bursting bubble of surface mirth, innocent of guile. And once she looked at me as I have been looked at in trains and restaurants, as though one quick glance, assessing the wrong tie and hair-cut, was quite enough.

I don't think it was a demonstration for me at all. I believe Sarah had come with us on the off-chance of being able to try out this performance, watching her technique in it, and watching Lady Strathlaird for that slight flicker in pale eyes which would be comment on a slip-up.

I remembered then what Edna had said about Sarah as an actress. Edna was wrong, she was probably clinging to an earlier judgment, perhaps from an active jealousy. Edna might even have been the threatened queen. Certainly Sarah was still a learner, and wore the sign, but she had technique and a passionate urge to put it to use. I could suddenly see her in my world, the wife of a perambulating American oil man, with all that she needed for the externals of this acquired in a week, and nothing more to learn. It gave me a cold feeling. Right then I didn't want to go on watching.

I made a move towards Gracie and Joe, and then checked that. They were surrounded by children, their own three and some others. Joe looked just a shade plump and gauche in a suit his wife had almost certainly bought for him, and which had been hanging in a cupboard for a long time. He was here because he had been brought, and his manner was a sullen, continuing protest. Gracie looked furious. She was eating a sandwich as though desperate for sustenance.

Those pompous stairs were flanked by passages leading down to windows. I could see a view and I thought a hint of water. I wanted to confirm this, that the view from the house had been carefully organized and maintained, too, including water and hills. I went down the passage.

The sun had come out. It looked almost warm beyond those

french windows; there was a terrace with urns and a formal garden down a flight of steps. I was just going to reach down for the handle when Sir Roger said, at my elbow:

'Hello. Going to have a look at our view, eh?'

I felt caught, we weren't supposed to go beyond the hall, but he was amiable about it.

'Let's go out, shall we? Rather nice, really. The house was well-sited. Sun pours in. Great help these days.'

It was quite comfortable on the flagged terrace, and a quick inventory of the view showed me that Sarah had been perfectly accurate; there were hills, well-wooded, a corner of a loch glistening, some fields, but no houses. You felt that houses simply wouldn't have been allowed. In England there would have been the village with the church spire, but not here; this was a panorama, with breadth and depth.

Then I saw smoke, a trickle of it beyond trees. Someone else did live within this view.

'Is that a cottage by the water?'

Sir Roger laughed.

'Oh, you've spotted that. Used to be my keeper, actually. Haven't got one now. Rent the place. To a writer. Odd type. Scottish Nationalist. Beard and kilt. And his name is Jones. I'll say this for him, he pays his rent, though I don't know where he gets the money. Writes plays in Lallans, though he talks with a Glasgow accent. His wife's a nice little thing, poor creature. He goes off a lot and leaves her with the two kids. We think it's a bit hard on her, but she doesn't seem to mind at all. She makes pots, you know, with clay and so on. Gave us one; it's in the hall. Can't say I like it myself but I'm told they sell in arty-crafty shoppes, you know.'

We were silent for a moment.

'I enjoyed your party,' Sir Roger said suddenly. 'Has that chap Bidacker flown off?'

'Yes, the last I heard of him he was in Mexico.'

'Odd bird. See a lot of him?'

'Not a lot, no.'

Sir Roger laughed.

'You don't mind, eh? You know, he's a bit loud. That's why I was louder. Look here, you must come out some time in summer.'

I was doing all right, two invites to Cambenden and not on bus days.

'Are you seeing the country at all? I mean you're not just spending your time footering back and forth to Edinburgh, are you? Because you really should get out while you're here. North or west. Now that's an idea. West Highlands. Been there?'

I told him I was going soon. He was interested.

'Islay, eh? Dullish, I find. Good whisky. But this is better to look at. I'll tell you a place, though, and you can get to it from Islay. Gigha. Seven or eight miles long, about a mile wide. You can spend the day, walk down it. If it's sunny you'll never forget it. Little paradise. Splendid estate management, too. Almost a model of how to do things out there. Don't meet it very often.'

Again we were silent, looking at Sir Roger's view, until he told me this country was damp, that it gave him rheumatism, that one had to stay by inherited acres, but he really preferred the bleaker east coast which was cold and dry.

I fancied I could smell wood-smoke from the hidden cottage. Suddenly there was a noise, distant, but penetrating and shrill, carried on the wind, a wailing.

'That's it!' Sir Roger shouted. 'Hear the damn' thing? Your blasted diesel cars! That's one of 'em!'

Ten

On the plane to Islay I knew just how much I was in love with Sarah Baillie. For the first time we were moving out from the insistent interruptions of our separate living. We were taking on the simplest, and yet with feeling, the most frightening of all experiments, being alone together through days in a place which would put the accent on that isolation.

When I got up in the morning it was to fog lying heavy over the Forth-Clyde valley, and I didn't want to go. I didn't want to go away for a set time during which I would have the opportunity to sleep with Sarah, the occasion carefully set ahead of us, almost the hour down on a schedule. It's fine if you just want a woman; I didn't.

She sat beside me, in by the window, and we both looked out. The Scottish air services, without very far to go, don't climb high. We were perhaps up four thousand, coming out from an ugly bit of moorland to the Clyde, with Bute and Cumbrae and Toward Light, and a lot of traffic on this wide estuary of the river. There was a liner, probably going to America, as glittering and unreal as something in a travel poster, but beyond it, modest and small, were houses, most of them white. The houses thinned out from a town and became isolated, but were always there; beyond some swelling of mountain more fields and more whitewashed stone.

It was May and the Scottish sun is then sharp and cool,

and the colours with it. It shone down on a land of tidy, moderate dimensions, of change within small compass, of packed detail that is almost like the detail of Japan, but without any touch of the precious.

We passed over the tip of Arran, and the island seemed to sit heavy beneath us, a great weight of rock displacing sea. One of its peaks had stripped into shreds an isolated, drifting quilt of cloud. Beyond this island was more mainland, the long arm of it which stretches down towards Ireland like a barrier against the Atlantic. Just in sight, almost on our horizon was Islay, blurred by mist, but open to the ocean. Down below, the waves became white flecked.

The day had a kind of glassy perfection set in brightness that was oddly mocking. We were both of us a hint furtive, with our purpose as neatly packed as our baggage. I'm a fussy packer, and for some reason I was quite certain then that Sarah was too, that you lifted a lid and saw an arrangement of articles carefully set out according to a long-established system. It was out of character for the actress, for the careless temperament, but then she wasn't careless.

It's not often these days that you keep low enough in a plane to have any sense of contact with the country you're passing over. You look down and see a pattern, and though, over mountains, you can be made nervous, the scale is a small one and you are high above the map, being projected from point of take-off to destination. But not on this flight. It wouldn't have really surprised me if someone had come out in front of one of those white houses and waved a table-cloth as a signal for the bus to drop down and pick them up.

'There's your island,' Sarah said. 'Have you done any checking up on your ancestors? Or are you leaving that until we land?'

'I'm leaving that until we land.'

I knew she was looking at the side of my head. Suddenly her hand slipped over mine.

'Sweetie,' she said. 'Cheer up!'

I turned and looked into her eyes. Then I began to laugh,

and so did she. We sat there quietly giggling, feeling much better.

The airport on Islay is an old R.A.F. landing ground converted, and we came down on to bumpy tarmac. I wasn't out of the plane before I heard the Gaelic, an old woman in front of us shouting out to people who were meeting her. The foreign tongue in Britain gave me an odd feeling, almost making me look around for the custom-shed. But there were only a few cars, a bored pilot, and a bald-headed man in a check tweed suit coming towards us.

His name was Allcott-Price and he came from Purley, and he ran the hotel into which we were booked. We were scarcely into his station wagon before he began to tell us about the big moment in his life when he had shaken off austerity England and come here. He had a kind of bluff joviality with a whine behind it, and he called me 'old boy' in every second sentence.

'We haven't a cook, I'm afraid, old boy. My wife's doing it just now. Hope to get one before the season really starts. Have one promised, you know. But I'm damned if that means a thing out here. She'll probably go off to Glasgow at the last minute. You can't count on 'em, really. Odd place. My home now, of course. Been here ten years, old boy.'

He thought about that, unhappily, driving fast. I could see the side of his face, sagging.

Sarah was looking out at peat bog. It was brown and ugly, with some of the peat cut and stacked. We could see nothing but that bog and a straight road ahead, with some rather ineffective looking hills rising up behind the moor.

When I saw the hotel I just wouldn't believe it. It sat with brown bog all around it and looked like a farm someone had given up in despair about the time my ancestors moved off to the States. The suggestion of dereliction reached us from a quarter of a mile away, and the impression wasn't relieved when we were de-bussed on some roughly strewn gravel by the main door.

The building was solid enough, a façade in stone two stories high, with a little closed-in porch projecting out in the middle.

Over this hung the skull and antlers of a seventeenth-century deer. That was about all there was in the way of decoration.

To one side was the remains of a garden, with rose beds, in which all the bushes seemed to be bent over towards Glasgow. Allcott-Price must have seen me looking.

'Haven't got a man for outside at the moment, old boy. But we've got plans for all this. My wife wants a terrace along the front here, you know, flagged and what not. Umbrellas and white furniture. Spot of colour and so on. We'll get it one day.'

I just didn't believe him. Neither did Sarah from the look of her.

'I thought you got a brochure about this place?' she hissed.

'I did. It sounded wonderful. Somewhere back there is a mile of golden sand.'

Sarah just looked at me. Then she reached down for the smallest of our four bags.

'I don't think there's any use waiting for the porter, Ned.'

But the porter came forward.

'Here, let me, old boy,' said Allcott-Price.

He registered us in as well, in our own names, two single rooms in the west wing. On the stairs he told us that the hot water reached its best about 6 p.m. And in a passage he banged open a door to reveal a most splendid modern bathroom in pale pink and black.

'We put this in, old boy. Should have seen what was here before. Had to get all the fixtures out from Glasgow. Would you believe it, when everything was in we couldn't get ruddy taps. Had to wait months for them. Right in the middle of my season, too. Well, here you are.'

That was me. Sarah was farther on, her voice diminishing, and Allcott-Price not calling her old girl.

My room was furnished in knobby Victorian with golden syrup finish. When I tested the bed with one hand the springs squeaked horribly and I unpacked thinking that the good things in this life never happen as a result of planning and keeping to schedules.

At 1 p.m. there was a clanging from lower regions and I met Sarah just as she was coming out of her door. She had changed and put on a lot more make-up than was normal, which was in sharp contrast to these surroundings. She looked at me without a word and in a complete silence we walked to the dining-room.

This was large, chill, and filled with the faint smell of tinned tomato soup. The windows provided a view of brown bog on the one hand and the prostrated rose bushes on the other. Against glass, and in a white light, sat the only two other occupants of the room, both young, darkish, and with that air of self-conscious misery which at once suggested a honeymoon.

'Do you want the view?' Sarah asked as we paused by a set table. 'Personally I prefer the fly stains.'

We sat, and long before soup reached us I was sharply conscious of being under observation. The honeymooners were looking us over, doing a bit of assessing and coming to conclusions that probably weren't going to be very complimentary. I knew that I had only to open my mouth and the whole situation would be clarified for them, a recurring situation in Britain these days, even in the remoter parts, a G.I. in disguise out looking for a quiet spot with his town cutie.

'Do you like tomato soup?' I said loudly. 'If you don't, there's fruit juice. It doesn't say what kind.'

The table in the window achieved then a deep, localized silence. That was something over.

A door burst open and through it sailed the waitress. We were both able to see her at the same moment. She was a honey blonde, and could have been Norwegian, big, lush, handsome and proud of everything she had. Almost without doubt she had descended from a roving Viking. I remembered that once Islay had belonged to them, a petty Norse kingdom, and this was one of their daughters, as splendid and over-powering as a *prima donna* in the days when it was considered necessary to carry meat in order to fatten up your voice. She loomed over us, amiable, white teeth flashing.

'Well?' she said, with the gentle lilt.

Sarah was crisp.

'I'll miss the soup. Is the fish fresh?'

'Aye, today. It came on the plane, you see. From Aberdeen.'

'You mean it isn't always?' I asked.

'It's not always,' Brünnhilde agreed.

She was quite charming, she had my smile, but not Sarah's.

'What about the meat?' I asked.

'Well, that's very nice today, too. It came on the plane from Glasgow as well, you see.'

'What do you do when the planes get storm-bound?' Sarah wondered.

'Och, we suffer,' said Brünnhilde looking at another girl with the kind of tolerance she could afford.

The last course was called baked cottage pudding and Brünnhilde produced it without apology but she did offer compensation. Again we got her splendid smile.

'Would you be wanting to go to a *ceilidh* tonight? There's one in Bowmore.'

'A what?'

'It's a kind of party, Ned. Open to the public up to a point. I think not, thank you, not tonight. What is your name?'

'Mairi.'

I was a little disappointed. As a name it sat too lightly on her. It even had a whiff of Barrie about it.

'Och, well,' said Mairi, 'there'll be another tomorrow night in Port Ellen if you'd like to go to that. Coffee?'

'Thank you, yes.'

'That's in the lounge.'

We went into the lounge. The honeymoon couple were before us, established in two chairs flanking a minimum fire. The rest of the room offered much less comfortable accommodation and the young man seemed suddenly to acknowledge this, with a kind of bitterness. He heaved himself about without actually getting up.

'Would you . . . ah . . . like to sit here by the fire . . . ah . . . Miss . . . ?'

They must have checked up in the register, deftly, on their way through.

'No thanks. I'm not cold.'

Sarah was staying off on her iceberg too long. It was irritating.

'What's the afternoon going to be like?' I asked, loudly.

The young man hadn't looked for this degree of intimacy between us. And it put his wife into a flat panic. She let the spoon slide off her saucer.

'Windy,' the man said. Then he improved on this. Military service had taught him to get on with all types, and the world was full of more things than you told your wife. 'Yes, I think definitely windy. It started before lunch.'

Sarah had lit herself a cigarette. She was looking at the wife, seeing the knitting tucked down beside the chair, and a pattern book.

'Are you from Edinburgh?' Sarah asked, with a sudden, easy sweetness.

That startled them. The young man admitted this, wondering how Sarah had guessed. She smiled again.

'Oh, I don't know. One of our worthies said that the Scots can never get away from themselves in their little country, and that's why they're so moral. Whereabouts in Edinburgh?'

'Newington, actually.'

'Well, I live right on the edge of it. Morningside, but very near Newington. You could throw a stone into Newington down the road.'

The young man flushed.

'You know it's odd. I . . . I think I know your face.'

'We probably used the same bus,' Sarah told him.

That afternoon we went walking in the wind, down to the golden sands. The Hebrides offer two kinds of winds, one of which is blowing most of the time, the first a breeze, in which you can just move around, the second a gale in which you can only lie flat. Our wind was force five going on to six. We couldn't talk and didn't try, but we got our exercise, the sort of exercise which is part of the British holiday religion, not rewarding in itself, but resulting in a kind of afterglow of virtue achieved.

It made us very hungry for the tea provided by Glasgow chain bakeries. We were eating it, in the lounge, when the door opened to admit the fifth guest. The honeymooners hadn't warned us, and it was a complete surprise.

'Well, well, *well!*' said Mr. Gruber. 'Here we all are. Here we all are!'

He was rubbing his hands, smiling, and was obviously a professional life and soul of. To meet one, out here in the middle of brown bog, was unnerving. The honeymooners simpered, I looked at him politely enough, but Sarah merely continued to put jam on a scone.

Mr. Gruber was travelling in animal foodstuffs and one of his proudest boasts was that he could break the social ice in any circumstances whatsoever. Thus challenged, Sarah put up a remarkable fight for it. Three-quarters of an hour later I would have said she was winning, but she looked at me, smiled and said:

'How about another walk, Ned?'

So we went out into it, this time towards the main road. A hundred yards from the hotel Sarah said:

'I know exactly how a slightly sensitive tart feels.'

'Sarah, I know this is bloody. We'll go in the morning.'

'Oh, it'll serve our purpose very well.'

'Will you shut up?'

'You mustn't think I'm upset in any way, Ned. Capri would probably have been better, but it's such a long flight.'

'Sarah!'

I caught her arm. She was nearly crying.

'I thought on the plane that . . .'

'I know, Sarah. Listen, use this place to learn your part. Stay up in your room, if you like. Or walk alone. We'll leave it like that. I'm a planner, I guess. What you hoped I wasn't.'

'What will you do?' she asked.

'I'll walk in the bloody wind!'

Sarah caught the lapels of my coat.

'Oh, Ned, my sweet. I feel all right again. In fact, more than all right. I'm ready for Grubers and honeymooners. Let's make a night of it.'

'What do you mean by that?'

'We'll probe Gruber to his depths. There's nothing cruel about it, he'll love it. We'll charm out his maximum. We'll make him purr. There ought to be a good whisky in the hotel. It's up to you to get it.'

Mr. Gruber, replete with an allegedly five-course dinner, and his triumphs at it, entered the lounge behind us all, but close behind.

'If you wish,' he said, 'I could render you a little Choping.'

He did, too. The comedy hour was over. With full stomachs we were ready for some spiritual food. He sat down at the piano, lifted the lid, and began what he called a 'mazoorka'.

It may be that animal feed and Chopin don't mix, and certainly that piano was a long way from a tuner, but for a moment or two I still couldn't believe that those sounds were meant, by their perpetrator, to have a serious intent. Then it was quite plain he was enjoying this other side to his personality. During a lull he explained that music was his hobby and that he sometimes sat at the piano alone for hours in his bungalow at Troon.

The young bride asked him about his feeling for Rachmaninoff and he said he had that as well, and proceeded to show us.

Sarah had slipped out of her part for a minute.

'The way you look,' I whispered, 'is the way Mary Queen of Scots must have felt that night she landed at Leith from France.'

The social worker smile jerked on to Sarah's face again. She put out her hand for the bottle.

It was a wonderful whisky, distilled on the island, and untouched by any blender. I'm not usually fond of the peaty West whiskies because they need their own water, but tonight we had that, and the whisky, even moderately indulged, put a transparent screen between us and the Rachmaninoff, followed by selections from Gilbert and Sullivan. During these the bride, supported by several sherries, really relaxed and she sang in a curious little reedy voice that was not unpleasing, thin but true. Gruber, considerate as ever, went *pianissimo* for the accompaniments. The groom sang, too. Finally I found myself singing.

The door opened and in came Allcott-Price, prodding his wife whom we saw for the first time, a sad little woman who looked as though the local wind would blow through her, released now on a brief parole from her sentence to a slow combustion cooker. It turned out that she could play a squeeze-box, and after two sherries she was persuaded, wearing all the time one of those cadaver smiles you see on the faces of new-comers to television who have been told to look lively. She even moved about a bit, jerking her bones.

When we could at last escape with decency from the thing we had helped to create, Sarah and I went for our third walk. It was Allcott-Price who mentioned the fact that there was a moon.

'We'll leave the door on the latch, old boy. The only thing you ever lock up out here is your whisky.'

We got out to find the wind had dropped and the night surprisingly mild, if you were wearing an overcoat and gloves and a Norwegian string vest, which I was. The moon beckoned us towards the sea and we went that way. After a little time Sarah tucked her hand into mine.

'A night to remember,' she said. 'You'll sleep well after all this exercise.'

'That's right.'

'Mrs. Allcott-Price whispered that she'd popped bottles in our beds.'

'We're good mixers, aren't we, Sarah? They like us. You get the feeling we're the kind of people they want to see coming back year after year. Jolly.'

'You've got the word, darling.'

'A place like this would grow on you in time. Or don't you feel it?'

'The only thing I feel, Ned, is a pain in the pit of my stomach. I think it's the cheese savoury.'

'I'll let you have my hot water bottle. Then you can have one on your stomach as well as at your feet.'

'The way you give,' Sarah said.

We went down on the sand. It was soft and shifting and we couldn't hold hands any more. I could see Ireland over Sarah's shoulder, suddenly as a cloud lifted from the moon. It was down there, long and low and glittering dully. She turned to me and I caught her and it became the kind of kiss that had been postponed a long time.

I didn't know why she was afraid, or why I was. I wanted to show that it didn't matter. She hung on to me, the pair of us padded like Eskimos. Her mouth twisted against mine and then was free by my chin.

'Oh, Ned, do they expect us to creep?'

'Does it matter?'

'Oh . . . I looked at those two. The holy state. Are they in love? Do they . . .?'

I tried to take her lips again, but she kept turning her head.

'Ned, maybe I'm wrong.'

'We're all wrong, all the time.'

'No . . . don't make it too easy for me. With you I feel . . .'

'Yes?'

'That I'm cheating. You don't deserve it. You want all those things. Things you ought to have.'

'I'll take anything on the book with you.'

'Don't say it like that, please! Don't sound like a bloody G.I.!'

'Sarah, I was scared coming here. Because I wanted so much more. I still want it.'

'I know! Don't you think I do? Why do you think I feel sort of . . . sick?'

'Stop it, Sarah. There's no need to shiver like that. You don't have to. . .'

'Let's go back!'

'The party will still be on.'

'I don't care. They won't hear us.'

We went back and in the door under the antlers. From the lounge came the laughter and Gruber's voice. He was the comic again. They might even have another session of song after that. We went up the stairs. I was a little behind Sarah.

'There's no need to go to your room,' she said in the passage.

So I didn't. I closed the door of hers behind us, and started to get out of the padding, the upper layers. She went over and dropped her coat on the bed and then went and stood at the dressing-table.

'The lighting in here is terrible,' she said.

I turned and found the switch by the door and clicked it up. With the curtains drawn it was pitch black, you couldn't see anything.

'Ned!'

I heard her moving towards the door.

'Leave it off, Sarah!'

'Oh.'

In a few moments, when I touched her, she gave a cry, soft in the darkness. I lifted her and held her against me hard, using my mouth. It took a long time for feeling to come to her, and then we had it, the tenderness that is awkward and frenzied and you both think will go on for ever, but really only happens once.

Eleven

In the morning we went to look for my ancestors. It was quite an excursion, which involved hiring Allcott-Price's wagon to take us in to Port Ellen. We took in the bride and groom, too, who seemed a bit dulled down after their night of dissipation, but in the town we lost them and were on our own, hunting.

Sarah had all the right ideas; she took me straight to the local church registry which we were shown by an elder because the minister was away. I had dates and names and finally we came to the one I was looking for, but in an odd context, a death notice for Morag MacDonald, wife to William Ewen MacDonald of Kilbarcher.

'I didn't know he buried a wife in Scotland,' I said. 'He had two in America.'

Sarah looked at me, and so did the elder.

'Och, well,' the elder said, 'some of them was long-lived men, indeed. Even in those days. That'll be the man you want all right.'

'Where's this Kilbarcher?'

'That's not easy to tell you, now. Oh, I know where I think it would be. But it was made into an estate, you see, and there's no crofts there now, and there hasn't been for a hundred years. Indeed, it could well be that your relation left from a clearance. We had boats in this harbour here to take the people from the crofts to America. There was an awful lot of people put off Islay. There's a song about it that we sing.'

'But there must be traces. A stone house doesn't disappear in a little more than a century.'

'No. That's true enough. Not left to itself it doesn't. But there was factors like madmen in those days. The men of the landowners they was. It was not enough to drive our people out of their houses, and burn them. The very stones was not left one upon the other.'

It gave me an odd feeling, the way that was intoned, the sense of wrong still continuing, the issue alive yet. You could see it was felt.

I'd never thought of my great-grandfather caught in a fury on this quiet island. I'd never thought of him at all. But I went out into the churchyard to look at the grave of his first wife who had never seen America, and we found it all right, a lettered stone, with no comment, just her name and the moss covering part of it. It was Sarah who found a handkerchief and rubbed off moss, so we could read the letters.

Kilbarcher wasn't going to be easy to find, only a direction, a glen on an old map. There was a road part of the way that led by one of those vast, turreted early Victorian mansions that the landowners put up after they had cleared an area of the encumbrance of men. The place had been well laid-out, to face south to a view, with trees and a walled garden. It looked empty now, almost derelict.

Sarah and I began to walk on grass, in the warm sun. And out beyond us, over rocks, was the sea, shining, calm, bounded by the mainland on which were the flecks of white stone houses.

'There's still a kind of road,' Sarah said. 'You can feel it.'

I couldn't.

'There on that bank,' she said. 'Look at the way it's cut out. And those were fields. You can still see where it was ploughed.'

She smiled at me. We were drained of questions, even of the routine uncertainties of a relation. Any place would have given us a kind of common denominator in living that day, but I was glad it was here and I knew she was, too.

'Three wives, eh?' Sarah said, and laughed. 'I wonder if he was sentimental like you? Out in America did he remember Morag? Or was he too busy getting on? I suppose he ended up with a thousand head of cattle?'

'I don't think so. Cash has always been a bit short in my family until recently. He didn't found any empire out in Texas. In fact he didn't move there until nearly the end of his life. That's all I know.'

'That and what you found out today. The first love. Have you been in love often, Ned?'

'I've thought I was once or twice.'

'And now?'

'Now I don't think I knew what it meant.'

She came in close to me, both of us walking.

'I take that to heart,' she said.

We had to go down into the glen and we went on a kind of grass-covered trail which had once been more than that, a track for carts. The little valley was really something cut out of low hills by a stream, but farther on it widened and there was room for fields, and we could see the long mounds of cultivation under the thick grass. There were a few sheep, and one stone retaining wall that was newish, as well as a pattern of older ones, half-covered, that had lost their meaning. We didn't find any trace of the house for a long time, and it was Sarah who began to search around under a bright green rowan growing out of a tangle of brambles. We found it there, a shape under the cover of bushes, the break for a door, the stones round about heaped and grass-hidden and fallen away from each other, but some of them hewn.

I knew it was Kilbarcher. I hadn't expected it to mean a thing, but it did, suddenly and sharply on a May morning in Scotland on an island I had only come to because of proddings from my mother. Probably I was in the kind of emotional state for it to mean something, but I was conscious of time as a space, so short in summers and the winters following, so long in the living of the people who saw them.

'Do you feel the ghosts?' Sarah asked.

And I knew what she meant. There are always ghosts in an old country, that sense of place used, of a vast pattern of human living behind what may now seem wilderness. Here was a little fragment of the pattern, so faint we had to hunt for it, nearly obliterated, but not quite.

'They didn't look at this view,' Sarah said. 'Not from the cottage anyway. They faced this bank for shelter from the wind.'

We found the well for Kilbarcher. A well in Scotland isn't something you have to dig down, it's just water coming bubbling out of rock, and all you do is deepen the pool and edge it, and it's ready for buckets. At this well was a black, wet stone hollowed out by feet like a threshold. It would take long enough to do that, people coming to this well and standing always in the same way as they bent over for water.

'He would have a boat,' Sarah said. 'They needed their fish.'

We went down the sloping valley to a small crescent of cobbled shore where there was no sand at all. Long ribs of rock slanted out on the half-tide and between these were two passages of deep water, tricky to get in and out of, because at all tides there would be a line where the sea foamed.

Maybe they didn't look at views in those days, but we did, over across water with a duller tone than the sky above it to the point of Kintyre, and Ireland again with Rathlin Island off its coast, the island offering the small mystery of a contained world we would never see.

We sat on cobbles and were shut off by that sound of the tide lifting and coming in towards us.

'He'd have to pull the boat well up here,' Sarah said.

'You talk as though you knew all about it.'

'We all have ancestors who lived like this. And not so far away.'

It didn't seem so far away and I'd never imagined it could come near me at all. Perhaps it was the simplicity of the pattern, the square of stones, the well, and the sea that didn't change.

'I don't expect they felt the peace we think we see,' I said.

'It was hard, yes. You came here young and you were probably carried away with your hands twisted like claws. But I think we can give them their peace. There was nothing they didn't know.'

'How do you mean?'

'They saw the limits of their world. And that was that. And you could be certain within the limits.'

I thought of the terror of that boat waiting in Port Ellen to take the evicted to America. It's not our kind of fear at all, but I could grasp at it now, the known world with its horizons set, and beyond it nothing you had ever really thought about. Then suddenly you were moving, pushed into emptiness.

Sarah jerked her head towards me. She spoke as though she had been following my thought, reading it.

'He must have envied Morag that day,' she said. 'Already in the churchyard.'

We did what Sir Roger had told me to do and went to Gigha for the day. I've seen a lot of small islands, and I'll see a lot more, but Gigha is the one I'll remember, green under sun, fringed by warm-coloured rocks with the sea lacing up to them. It is only about seven miles long and one wide, and it lies near to the main Kintyre coast, so near you can see the cars running along a highway. But it still has the feeling of isolation, not remote, just a little world folded into itself under a rising lip of ground that keeps off the destructive Atlantic winds.

We climbed down a rope-ladder from the steamer for a landing at the north end. It was quite early in the morning, no haze yet in spite of a day settling for heat. In the little boat bumping up and down was a man at the oars and another standing waiting to help us. The man looking up was like a pirate, jet black hair, swarthy, grinning, cynically amused. He must have helped dozens of female tourists into his little boat, not all of them wearing trousers.

Sarah jumped and he caught her, holding her a bit longer than he needed to, I thought. He turned with her in his arms and put her down on a seat. He looked up at me and said, 'Watch it, then.' I landed on floorboards and looked up to see Sarah grinning at me.

The rower pushed off from the steamer, the pirate sank down to hold the tiller, and we moved slowly away on a morning tide, rising and falling.

I felt that almost always mistaken compulsion to talk to people who are doing something for you.

'Do you meet all the steamers this way?'

'Only when we know there's people coming off. They phone us from Port Askaig.'

'So you can't just suddenly decide to land on Gigha?'

'Not at this end. No you cannot.'

He spoke politely enough, but like an adult to a child known not to be very bright. And then suddenly the Gaelic began to flash past Sarah and me where we sat side by side, the rower calling out something and the pirate bellowing an answer and rocking with laughter. I thought I caught something like 'Yank' but I couldn't be sure; perhaps they haven't got a word for us in the Gaelic, we were invented so late.

Sarah produced cigarettes and passed them around. The rower stopped rowing and we just drifted, the steamer a long way off now. She was thanked politely, the packet and matches handed back. The pirate lolled in his seat, one foot in a rubber shoe up against the oarlock holder. He watched us with a kind of quizzical, deliberate interest. I was quite certain that Sarah was aware of him as more than a boatman, and thought he probably approved of hair as black as his own. She seemed to keep on smiling, and it might have been at the morning and sun. I took her hand then and held it, with the feeling that at any moment her smile might move over into laughter, and black eyes were watching us all the time.

We landed in a cove against a rough stone jetty. I got out first and pulled Sarah up. There wasn't a house in sight, just a sandy track, and flat, open land covered in grass and flowers. The mild wind moved over wild orchis and they bent to it, small, exotic, their colours not of the north at all.

'We just go down this path?' I asked.

'There is only one,' the boatman said. 'There is no way to lose yourself.'

He wasn't moving and neither was the rower; the whole day seemed theirs, and they were quite content not to rush at it. I paid them and the pirate pocketed the money and sat back again.

'Well, let's get going,' I said briskly.

We got going, and I knew were watched out of sight behind a hummock.

'Where do they live?' I asked suddenly. 'There isn't a house or anything.'

'That's their problem,' Sarah said. She caught my hand. 'Just look at this.'

There was a lot to look at; Ireland in the distance, Islay out in the Atlantic with the twin peaks of Jura sliding in behind it, and in the clear light the colour glowed from sea and sky and the distant hills. It was a morning with the music behind it of a gentle sea.

Then we heard something else, an engine. We had to get off the track to let the motor-bike past. It was plunging a bit in the sand, the rower in front, the pirate sitting behind with hands on his hips and a cigarette in his mouth. As they came up the pirate took out the cigarette, smiled, ducked his head and shouted, mocking, above the erratic explosions:

'Chee-ri-ooo!'

A little bit ahead the track firmed and they shot away. We still couldn't see a house or a sign of man, just the open flat land the Scots call *machair*, sharp green, spotted with colour, but without utility, no sheep, left to grass and to ten thousand flowers.

'How's Mary Queen of Scots getting on?' I asked.

'All right.'

'You mean you've been thinking about her?'

'Of course. Quite a lot.'

That gave me a jolt. I hadn't been thinking about the oil business.

'What have you been doing, worming your way into the part?'

'You could put it like that.'

'I should have thought learning the lines came first?'

'Oh, I know the lines.'

She sounded remote, almost a little irritated.

'You like the play?' I asked.

'Yes. You said something once about it being in the romantic tradition. I know what you mean now. It follows the dream. It doesn't challenge it in any way.'

'The dream can, of course, be right.'

Sarah shook her head.

'I wonder? In this Mary's the victim, and not really of herself. And I can't quite believe that. You see, I feel she was in terror from the moment she landed in Scotland. Oh . . . not the terror of someone afraid of physical danger. She had plenty of courage when it came to that. But the other kind of fear, of being committed to perpetual strangeness . . . that's what I mean. This country was always alien to her. I think it stayed that way, all the time, that after leaving France she never walked a road that was hers.'

We sat down, this time facing Kintyre and the white houses and cars on a long road. I was thinking about Sarah's village, and the comfort of it, of nothing ever happening that you couldn't foresee. And I saw what she was after in playing this part, Mary from the village of the Court of France, trying to make another one in a cold Scots palace, and never managing.

Little France . . . there's a place outside Edinburgh called that, designed for the people Mary brought with her. And only the name remains.

Sarah was looking at me.

'You think I have cheek, don't you, Ned? You think I'm a damn' bad actress.'

'How could I think that?'

'You've seen me in a studio. Doing a hack job with only a moderate degree of competence. What you saw was real enough. It wasn't just one of my bad days.'

She was very near me, and I could have touched her, but I
didn't.

'What are you getting at, honey?'

'Just that my norm is pretty bad. I don't need anyone else to
tell me, I can tell myself. But I have escaped from that norm.'

'You told me. And I believe it.'

'No, don't be too glib! It isn't easy. But it can happen.
And a man who knew it could happen said this:

If only, most lovely of all, I yield myself and am borrowed
By the fine, fine wind that takes its course through the chaos
    of the world
Like a fine and exquisite chisel, a wedge-blade inserted;
If only I am keen and hard like the sheer tip of a wedge
Driven by invisible blows,
The rock will split, and we shall come at the wonder. . . .

Do you know who wrote that?'

'Sounds like Lawrence.'

'Yes. He seems to be out of fashion. And I mayn't even have
his meaning. But you know what it says to me? That God in his
mercy can reach down to help, even a bloody mummer.'

'Sarah!'

'Sorry. I didn't mean to work myself up. But I was just
trying to explain how it can happen, how you wait for it to
happen. Work, of course, but it needs more than work. It
needs . . .'

'It needs what, honey?'

'I don't know. A kind of waiting, I guess.'

'And you want it to happen with your Mary?'

'It's a chance. It might be then. Come on, we've got a good
way to walk. And then we'll have to get a meal.'

We came to a road and the first house, a pretty house,
freshly whitewashed and sitting in a garden. It was under that
lip of rising ground to the west and the fields were sheltered,
and the whole place looked like it could hide from the wind on
a stormy night and hold quiet.

'Ned, you're a little shocked, aren't you? My good practical Ned sees me caught up in a delusion. Is that what you feel?'

How could I tell her that I suddenly felt alone?

'It's a long way from me,' I said. 'What's the use of my waiting for any fine wind?'

'Oh. You think I'm a fool. Darling, don't hate the fool.'

'Will you stop talking like that!'

'All right. It's not a day to talk like that.'

We had lunch in the inn, half-way down the island. They weren't expecting visitors and hadn't much to give us, they said, but they gave us something I'd never had in Scotland, half a well-hearted lettuce each, just taken from the garden, and tomatoes still sun-warm and cucumber and cold meat. And the woman with a quiet voice baked some scones for us and put down her own butter. When we went out again it was hot, really hot.

The road was dusty and we left it to wander down to the shore with hours to wait for our boat at the south end. We found a cove, without much sand, but shade under rocks if we needed to move back into it, and we lay down to hear the gulls and the sea.

'I'd like to swim,' I said. 'But I'd sink after all those scones.'

'You can't swim.'

'Why not? You mean because we haven't brought anything to keep us modest? There's no one here.'

'There's always someone here in the Highlands.'

'Sarah, are you going fey or something?'

'No, Ned, but this isn't the great open spaces. The Highlands are no place to be private in, out of doors. You think you're miles from men and look up suddenly into the eyes of a shepherd. Or a hitch-hiker. Don't try to make love to me, I won't let you. After all, you're not being frustrated. Our hotel could have been designed for creepers, with that wind howling all the time.'

There seemed to be no wind on Gigha. I lay back and closed my eyes and put out my hand for Sarah's, feeling her fingers tightening on mine. I slept, and when I woke, Sarah was sitting up, her arms around her knees, her hair fallen forward. She looked as though she had been staring at the sea, and then stopped and bent her head. While I watched her she lifted it again.

'Ned, there's a little black thing swimming.'

'What?'

'It's not a seal. I thought it was, but it's too small. Look.'

I saw it all right, something swimming fast, very tiny, like a bird's head out of the water, a black head. And then it began to come in towards us.

'Some kind of seabird,' I said. 'Could be a guillemot. Looks like it's coming in for a visit.'

But the seabird seemed to be swimming now with a sort of despairing burst of speed. It was queer to watch. It had been going in a straight line, but switched to a zigzag. Then, with a flutter of wings, the first big black-backed gull dropped. It seemed to land right on the small black head.

'Ned! That gull's attacking it!'

'There's nothing we can do, Sarah.'

'But it's horrible. There's another gull! It's such a little bird!'

It was a little bird, desperate now. The gulls rose out of the water to circle fifty feet up and then drop. We saw the splash, a fluttering, a beak slashing out.

'It hasn't a chance, Ned. Why do they . . . ?'

I didn't say anything. Sarah got up and went down to the water's edge. She picked up a stone and threw it, and it was ridiculous, the gulls never even noticed. No one could throw a stone anywhere near them.

'It's still swimming! Ned, it dives and goes under water.'

The gulls rose and waited and then, when the black head came up again, they dropped.

'Oh, damn those brutes! If I had a gun! They pull the eyes out of new-born lambs.'

The black bird stayed under water a long time now. Then suddenly it came up and wasn't attacked. It was much nearer us, a squat head, and still swimming. The gulls seemed to have completely lost interest and were floating on the gentle waves with folded wings, serene. More lighted on the water, and the seabird was able to move through them, coming in towards the shore, right towards us.

'He's got away, Sarah. Come and sit down. If it's a guillemot he may come in and land.'

It was a guillemot and he did come in, almost drifting. In the clear water we could see his feet kick out now and then. Finally he touched the stones and rose on them, a little miniature penguin, solemn, very quiet.

'He sees us, Ned. If I go down . . . ?'

'If you move he'll go away.'

But she had to go. The little bird flopped off and into the water again. He swam quite strongly, out along the edge of rocks, away from us. He disappeared.

'He looks a bit punch-drunk,' I said. 'But he's survived.'

An hour later Sarah was asleep. The tide was coming to the full, pushing back seaweed. I'd been watching the opposite land and the sky, with a few clouds in it. Then I saw the guillemot.

The tide was bringing him this time, without any help from those kicking legs. The bird was on his side, floating, quite unmarked, very neat, very small, and dead.

I was careful to make no sound as I got up and went down to the water. I didn't want Sarah to know the bird was dead, and I lifted it out and put it under a heap of seaweed. What I felt as I did that was silly and sentimental, but I went on feeling it.

Twelve

I DIDN'T forget Sarah's reference to mummers and the mercy of God. A small, half-furtive sense of outrage continued in my mind; I couldn't adjust at all to what seemed now a spurt of emotionalism on her part, something quite undisciplined by reason. The Protester likes to pretend, at any rate, that he always has reason for company, and, from reason, a nice set of fairly tidy regulations.

Sarah was by-passing all the regulations. If she really believed there was available to her on occasion a power that was superhuman, she was being too casual about approaching this power. There had to be a pattern of discipline by which it could be induced, something more than just waiting.

Certainly I had to admit that she hadn't suggested you could turn on the mercy of God like a tap, but this was apparently as far as her theology went, and to my reasonably tidy mind this seemed inexcusable. I was reminded, not pleasantly, of hearing a celebrated British actor say on the radio that before he went on stage he always prayed to the actor's god, whoever he might be.

That had shocked me, just as Sarah had really shocked me. The actor, and Sarah, were dissociating themselves as individuals from the thing which they wished to create, hoping for some mysterious addition of power beyond their natural endowments. And furthermore I didn't see that they had really earned this power in any way. Were temporary spasms of so-called dedication enough to call it forth?

The very idea of this seemed to make nonsense of all the Saints as well as all the Protesters. My imagination wasn't elastic enough to make room for a kind of specialized mercy at all. I couldn't see it happening.

Perhaps my unease was increased by having had Lawrence quoted at me, for if any artist has ever made a fetish of having no regulations at all, he's the one.

You can be in love with a woman for a long time before you're interested in her. You don't have ever to get interested in her, but if it happens that you are pushed over the low barrier between the pleasures and real concern, then a sense of responsibility comes into it. And it's where love begins to get really painful.

I heard Sarah going over her part. We went down to the beach behind the hotel in the continuing days of sun, and I wasn't just being a kind of prompt-machine. I wanted to see just how far she could go as an actress in training herself. I suspected sloppiness now in detail, a tendency to sketch in the part she was creating and then to lunge at the emotions. It was oddly disturbing to me when this didn't happen.

We went over the thing again and again and again. Sarah's emphasis was on timing and the mechanics, as though at this stage she was deliberately leaving out a great deal, perhaps for Angus to put in. This was the dull business of technique, and I began to get bored superficially, but at the same time I had to give her the marks for thoroughness.

We had our moments together all right, mostly as the result of my creeping, but those sessions on the beach weren't exactly the oil man's ideal holiday. Here we were with the kind of climatic conditions which Scotland doesn't often provide for an idyll, and I was spending much of them saying the lines of Queen Elizabeth or Bothwell.

Sarah usually sat for her work, very rarely turning to me, mostly looking at the Atlantic. Sometimes she dug out the sand with one hand. When we had finished a scene she often lay back and shut her eyes.

Those were minutes of a sort of loneliness. I was becoming more and more conscious of her body, of the things in our love-making which provoked a response and those that didn't. We were already almost settling to a habit on a bed in which the initiative was more and more left to me, and I wasn't always successful. Sarah, naked in my arms, sometimes came near to that desertion where her attention was removed, and it was maddening. It gave me a feeling of complete incompetence. Once I nearly got up and did the creeping in reverse. She stopped me when I was angry, and that was better than it ever had been.

I thought, not without a hint of bitterness, that it might become like this in marriage, the seconds when you felt you were snatching again at the reasons for being together suddenly intruded on by domestic detail, one partner remembering about not having put out the gas after the milk nightcap. I was aware, too, of the idiot romanticism of the male which makes it so difficult for him to accept his sex as routine. He has to be, over and over again, the hunter, with that recurring moment of triumph in the woods.

Our eighth day wasn't quite so warm. The Scottish sun is never effective through even the thinnest of clouds, and these had come, from the sea, grey streamers that gave the sky a watery look. We found rocks to make a cup of shelter and sat closer. For the eighty-fourth time I was Queen Elizabeth, bitter, potent, removed from the common experience. Sarah, as the Queen wrecked by living, had said her last word and was silent.

I looked at the back of her head, at black hair falling over her neck. I put my fingers under it and she said sharply:

'Don't, Ned!'

'Sorry, wrong timing.'

Her head jerked round.

'What's the matter with you?'

'Don't worry about me. I'm just a dirty-minded old man.'

136

Sarah laughed.

'Full of yourself. I said that when we first met. Your cup of you reaches the brim all the time.'

'That calls for a sniff. Are we getting anywhere with our work?'

'I think so.'

'You know, Sarah, the more we go over this play, the more I like Elizabeth. I'm sorry to do this to the author when he's tried so hard to make her the deadly nightshade. But you can't push Elizabeth around. This final scene is the complete bunk.'

She stiffened.

'What do you mean?'

'It's bunk because Elizabeth had a mind that was more masculine than any male's. She didn't want any of the things that Mary had, her silly court, her husband of convenience, her lover with a hairy chest. You can't make Elizabeth envious of Mary and make it stick.'

'So you think this last scene is meaningless?'

'The sexual envy angle . . . yes. To Elizabeth Mary was just something to be dealt with when the time came. And that's exactly what happened.'

Sarah stood. She dusted the sand off her slacks. She looked at me again.

'It's odd, Ned, that this should strike you so forcefully just now. Perhaps I was the wrong cutie for you to take away for two weeks.'

Then she walked off, disappearing around rocks.

I didn't go back to the hotel for afternoon tea. A rising wind made me move, and I walked first along the shore and then up over a hill at the end of it from which I could see Port Ellen and the distilleries which made the smooth nectar. Another liner was off to America, gleaming with that painted insolence of the big ship in sheltered waters. Later on it could roll all right, but it wasn't admitting it now. There was a lighthouse across on another point of the island which had the appeal of all lighthouses, the carefully staged remoteness, the shine of whitewash against a place where nature roughens things up. I wanted to go on walking, but thought I'd better not. I could see Sarah sitting in the hotel lounge with one of the detective novels she had brought. She never studied her part after tea. The time had come then for relaxation.

Why does feeling make the detail of the beloved's habit loom so large? Why are we always peering at it and trying to fit it in with our own habits, busy making a whole where there have always been two parts and always will be?

I seemed to have no flair with Sarah for striking off the mood we could share and use together. She was still wary with me, not often relaxed. Oh, we had our laughter, we had a lot of things, but they didn't add up to any kind of total that looked neat.

Probably I had a lust for neatness, for things cut and dried, for religion with theology and sex with moments of splendour that could only be made by two imaginations, not one.

When I got back to the hotel the first thing I noticed as I hit the gravel piece was that the antlers of that deer which had starved to death a couple of centuries back seemed to be sagging to one side. And before I reached the door Allcott-Price came out of it carrying a pair of household steps.

'Oh!' he said, 'just fixing this. A nail's given way, old boy. They corrode frightfully in this salt air, you know. Nearly came down once before. On top of a dear old soul staying.'

'Interesting way to die.'

He looked startled.

'Oh, I don't think they'd actually kill anyone, old boy. Not as heavy as all that, you know. By the way, I think Miss Baillie has had some rather bad news.'

'What?'

'Well, you see, there was a phone call from Edinburgh this afternoon. They wouldn't leave any message. But they said it was most urgent that Miss Baillie call back at once. And would we find her? Well, I'm awfully sorry, old boy, but we're frightfully short-handed just now and we just can't go careering around the place looking for our guests. You do see that, don't you?'

'Why sure.'

'I thought Miss Baillie looked put out. But it may have been the news. Anyway she went to her room right after phoning up. She hasn't had any tea. I was wondering if we ought to keep it on the go.'

'I think you can write off tea today.'

'Righty-o, old boy.'

He clumped up those steps and began to sing, punctuating the lines with his hammer. He was singing that he was going to wash that man right out of his hair.

At Sarah's door I knocked. She was sitting in a straight-backed chair by the window, and beyond her the light was still firm, the brown moor and a corner of sea. She couldn't have been looking out.

'Sarah. . . ?'

'My mother's dead,' she said.

I shut the door quietly.

'Sarah, what can we do?'

She looked at me.

'I don't know. What *can* you do?'

I was startled to see how much she minded, the shock not even covering pain any more. She looked like someone who had been sitting quietly bolt upright on a chair accusing herself.

'Sarah, you told me it was something that could happen any time. You must have . . .'

'Please don't say that!'

'But you . . . can't blame yourself. I mean for being away. Is that what you're doing?'

'No.'

'Well what is it?'

'They sent for Eileen.'

'I don't understand, Sarah?'

'Neither did I for a few minutes. But mother's been bad for two days. Plenty of time . . . for me . . . I mean for me to get there. Plenty. . . . But they sent for Eileen!'

I caught her then. Her sobs came drawn up from her stomach.

'I was the one . . . Ned. I . . . I came home. I . . . I tried. Oh, God, I tried! And they . . . they sent for Eileen. Mother must have wanted . . . that.'

'Sarah! She didn't want to spoil your holiday.'

'No! No! No!'

'Sarah, stop making something that isn't there.'

'It *is* there! Oh, God, it is there!'

And suddenly I couldn't tell her it wasn't. I knew enough about the Baillies to guess at what she meant. Sarah had come home, and it was the dutiful gesture, and she'd meant it for more than that. But they had been suspicious, her mother and her mother's friends and probably her father, too. They looked for another motive more explicable in their living than the impulse of kindness.

I was certain that it wasn't duty which had brought Sarah home, but that she came back on a search for something of feeling amongst her own people, and her search had proved sterile. The sensible don't allow their affections to range outside the world they have devised for themselves, or inherited, a world with strict margins. Even to the climbers the margins are continuously real, you take the upward step carefully and then consolidate. The Baillies had climbed right out of the world in which Sarah had been brought up, but they had paused for that tucking in of the margins, making everything snug and secure.

Sarah had neither climbed with them nor wanted what they had when they got there. After the painstaking effort of years this was almost unforgivable. If your children desert it is a particular and intimate affront to your achievement. It wasn't the actress they minded in Sarah, it was the carelessness about their values.

And so the mother, who had made lovers of us in her mind long before we could have been, dying, had sent for Eileen.

I knew that I couldn't produce any acceptable comfort for Sarah, and so I went out and tried to find out about boats and planes. There was nothing more that day. We could leave in the morning from Port Askaig on the other side of the island, but we had to spend this evening and night in the weighted leisure of inaction when to be on the move is an end in itself.

Sarah came down to dinner and we listened to Gruber's jokes. He was in a particularly bouncing form, and had the honeymooners in stitches. As though suddenly conscious of being surrounded by the young caught up in an exploratory phase, he allowed himself to become a little *risqué* with his stories, the balding man of the world who knew a thing or two as yet beyond our experience. Gruber had travelled in whisky at one time and his life during this period seemed to have been a succession of gaudily coloured incidents reminiscent of What the Butler Saw.

It was Sarah who led the way into the lounge for coffee and music. She made no excuse about a headache and sat with a smiling composure which was horrible for me to see. And when she said, finally excusing herself, 'Don't you hurry away, Ned,' I felt as though she had slammed a door.

I didn't go to her room. Once I started, meaning to go along and knock, but I didn't do it. I had no way of knowing whether she needed me then or preferred to keep me out. I lay on my bed thinking that this might be the moment to push our relation on to a level of feeling it hadn't yet reached, that I might be able to show Sarah I was with her in a way she didn't guess.

But I didn't go. I just fell asleep.

Thirteen

I DIDN'T phone Sarah up until three days after Mrs. Baillie's funeral and I did it then from Grangemouth, so that it wouldn't seem as if I was pressing to see her. Sarah didn't come to the phone for a long time; it was answered by one of the women Mrs. Baillie had complained about. Sarah sounded calm and composed. I was the one who was apologetic.

'I know it's a bit soon to trouble you. It's just that I was wondering, Sarah, if I could do anything?'

'I don't think so, Ned.'

'You're . . . alone again, I suppose? I mean with your father?'

'No. Eileen hasn't been able to go back to school. She's here.'

'Oh. So you're still sort of tied?'

'Yes, I am rather.'

'Well . . . maybe I'll phone up again in about a week.'

'I doubt if I'll be able to see you. Eileen will still be here. She's under the doctor's care. It's a sort of nervous upset. Shock, mostly.'

'In that case, I'll wait until I hear from you. You've got my phone number here in Grangemouth?'

'Yes, Ned, I have it.'

'As soon as you can get out . . . you will use it won't you?

I mean even if it's only for an hour or two. It might help to get out in the car for a bit or something?'

'I'll look forward to that.'

'Sarah!'

'Yes?'

'What about your part? What are you going to do about that? Are you going on with it?'

'Yes. Rehearsals haven't started yet. I'll be ready when they do.'

'Sarah, I'm glad you feel that way about it. I mean, it's the only thing for you to do. I was afraid you might give it up.'

'Oh, no,' she said. 'That never entered my head.'

I didn't go up to Edinburgh for ten days after that talk with Sarah. I kept waiting for a call to come through to Grangemouth but it didn't. The only thing I did do was go round to Gracie's for supper one night, and Gracie had been quarrelling with Joe about money and they sat through the meal with Gracie being charming to her guest, Joe looking at his plate, and the atmosphere thick with that peculiar fug of domestic unrest. Even the kids played up to it; they yowled in turns. It was Joe who went out to quieten them down and he kept staying away a long time. Gracie filled in the intervals with trying to pretend that she wasn't sharply sorry to have me just at this moment. We all had one drink too many after doing the dishes and suddenly, in the middle of a story she was telling, Gracie burst into tears and got up and walked out.

Joe said, looking at the carpet:

'Would you like a cigar? I just got some in.'

'No thanks, Joe.'

'I guess I will,' Joe said bitterly.

He took a long time to get it going, and the room began to reek from explosive suckings. It may have been Havana, but it didn't smell top quality to me. In fact it might very well have been what they call over here an export reject. You could see that cigar wasn't going to help Joe one little bit towards the feeling that he was a man in control of his own destiny.

Words weren't something you really expected from Joe. He gave you his company sometimes with just a faint air of reluctance, but not much more. When he began to talk I knew that something was really gnawing. He looked at me. He had the technician's face, smooth to human suffering. Now it was crinkled.

'Do you save?'

'What, Joe?'

'I mean, do you save money?'

'I'm afraid so.'

'Every month?'

'Well, yes, I suppose so. I'm not really terribly extravagant about a lot of things.'

'You're not married, you mean.'

'It could be that I guess. Marriage brings a lot of commitments.'

Joe puffed.

'The thing that burns me up, Ned, is that we live in this little house at a rent that wouldn't get us a comfortable dog kennel back in the States. I know for a plain fact that my income is six times my neighbour on the left and five times my neighbour on the right. One has got two kids and the other's got three. They seem to eat and they wear clean shirts. And they go two weeks' holiday every year. Whereas I'm down the drain every month.'

'Joe, maybe you've got a lot more tied up in the future.'

'Sure, for the kids' college. And for that house we're going to get when we go back to the States. I tell you this, Ned, I'm scared to go back to the States. If we can't live on big money over here how the hell could we do it in America?'

'You'll get promotion, Joe.'

'Sure. Right now I'd like to be promoted to an island where the kids could wear palm leaves and all we need for housing was a couple of tents. Honestly, Ned, I get scared. Maybe I lose my temper. I guess you've seen what happens.'

'I wouldn't call Gracie extravagant.'

'It isn't Gracie. It's the overall picture.'

He sat then and stared at the overall picture against clouds of rank cigar smoke.

Gracie came in again. She had made up her face and looked perfectly calm.

'We've got some Drambuie,' she said. 'Shall I serve it all round?'

'Sure,' Joe agreed. 'And when you've filled up our glasses pour the rest on the fire. It's getting a bit clogged up.'

I left as soon as I could. I wouldn't have believed that Joe could erupt, but now I'd seen it. I'd also seen one of those acute phases of matrimonial distress which are always a little incredible to those who have never tied themselves up. On the face of it there's nothing surprising in the fact that two people who have undertaken to live together for the rest of their known time should come to moments when that prospect seems almost unbearable. But the singles can never quite get away from the idea that this shouldn't be, that there ought to be a kind of balance achieved which would help the pair to move gracefully over the sticky bits. I had always thought that Gracie and Joe had that balance, and I was quite simply startled that they could still hit the lows where neither was able to put on an act for the outsider.

To what point did this take the single in his pursuit of love? I went into a still-open pub, ordered half a pint of heavy Scots beer and thought about it. I was surrounded by males, pipe smoke and heavy, grumbled talk. It was about football, the pools and racing, a sexless atmosphere, smelling faintly of the Gents' quite near at hand.

I wondered if Gracie had shut the door after me and returned to Joe saying: 'Thank heaven the bloody man's gone!' Perhaps now they were facing each other, getting rid of pent up tensions, half-enjoying themselves, with the whole evening likely to end in bed in one of those occasions which give sharp point to the pleasure of matrimony.

The outsider just can't know. Doors are always shutting on him.

'Time gentlemen, please. Drink up now. Time!'

The barman had a broad, honest face and wore a blue and white striped apron. By this time I'd had quite a lot to drink.

'Are you married?' I asked.

'Eh?'

'Are you a married man?'

'Aye.'

He glared.

'What's it like?'

He wiped very big red hands on his apron. Then he leaned towards me a little.

'Listen, Yank, if you're wanting another beer you'd better order. And remember this, we don't have no drunks in this house.'

When I finally got up to Edinburgh I went along to the Melrose which I knew would be half-empty in the evening. Angus was there, sipping a gin. He'd taken to using a cigarette-holder and he looked like a man of substance slumming.

'Well, Ned!'

'How's the tycoon?'

He laughed.

'As well as can be expected. I'm not finding it all a push-over.'

'We've got to suffer for our advances in this world. What will you drink?'

'I've got a feeling I'm in your debt, Ned.'

'All right, a whisky.'

Angus had money now, but old Mother Broadcasting had taught him to watch it. Those coins crept across the counter as though they just hated to leave home.

'Hear you've been away,' he said. 'Testing the Highlands.'

One look at him and I knew he knew all about it. Probably the honeymooners on Islay had been cousins of his. You learn, living in Scotland, that privacy is anti-social, and furthermore any attempts to enforce it would deprive a lot of people of their major interest in living.

'We had beautiful weather,' I said.

146

'Hm. Lucky. Sad about Sarah's mother.'

'Yes. But I'm glad to know Sarah's going on with the play.'

'Oh, yes. I don't think she had any choice, Ned. She had to do something.'

'I . . . don't follow?'

'Haven't you been seeing her?'

'No, not for a time. Why?'

'Don't mean to tell me that you . . . well, don't know the full situation?'

'Supposing you let me have it and I tell you whether I'm in the picture.'

'About her father, Ned?'

'That doesn't ring any bells at all.'

'Good Lord! I thought somehow you'd know. I mean, seeing so much of them. . . . But then, of course, Sarah didn't know either.'

I waited. He was started, I knew that. There was no use trying to stop Angus enjoying himself in his own way. But something told me that this story fitted in with Angus, that it brought him a kind of comfort.

'Sarah's old man has been after another woman for years,' he said bluntly.

'After her? What do you mean by that?'

'I mean he wanted a divorce so he could marry again. A Mrs. Harris.'

'A Mrs. . . . ?'

I stopped. I remembered the lobby of the local Rep theatre, a tall woman in a cocktail hat, talking to Sarah, forcing that talk with a kind of determination. She was the woman who had made her first husband prefer another world.

'Angus, are you on the level with this?'

'My dear man, it's been known around the town for long enough. At least everyone in Baillie's crowd. Mrs. Harris is a very determined specimen.'

'I've met her. I met her with Sarah once. Sarah didn't know, I'm sure.'

'That's what I'm telling you; she didn't. We found that out. Of course she's been away.'

'But Mrs. Baillie was in her bed dying!'

'It started before that. That just held it up.'

'She knew?'

'Of course she knew. She refused to give her husband a divorce. She was fighting until she couldn't any more.'

I saw what he meant. The big woman had been forced to give up her fight. It had been stopped for her. After that it had just been a question of waiting, for her, and two others.

I thought of that house up in Morningside, the big house with the empty feeling that wasn't just something from the way the rooms were furnished. The old man ate his meals in his study, and Ella Baillie was upstairs with a tray and the television, and Sarah could have her friends into that big drawing-room that looked like it was never intended for human beings.

'Oh, God!' I said.

'This has been a shock for you.'

'Yes. I guess it has been. Look, Angus, I can't stay. I only came in for a minute. See you around.'

'Come into our rehearsals if you like. They start in a fortnight.'

'I might. Thanks.'

He knew where I was going. But it was good to get away from him, out into the summer night where people were walking around still dressed for winter.

I didn't think as I drove; there was a kind of block on anything I could think about. I just watched the road with the feeling all the time that Islay was a long way behind Sarah and me, pushed there.

There was no Daimler parked in front of the house, which looked black because shadow had fallen on it. Sarah came herself to answer my ring, Sarah in a grey dress that didn't suit her, the kind of thing a woman would buy and put away until a moment when she wasn't thinking about clothes.

She didn't ask me in, she stood back, as though accepting

148

my right to be there, or too weary to challenge it. She had put on a fire and that big television set was clicking away over a programme, not loud enough to be really heard, but making enough sound to cover silence.

'I've been talking to Angus,' I said.

Sarah opened a box and took a cigarette.

'And Angus told you about Mrs. Harris. What have you come to do, Ned?'

'To tell you I love you.'

She closed her eyes. Her hand, lifting with a lighter in it, fell again. She plucked the cigarette out of her mouth and threw it in the fire. Then she went over and stood there, one arm on the mantelpiece.

'Sarah, why are you in this house? Why do you have to stay here? Don't try to tell me it's your home!'

'No, it's not my home. But I have to stay because Eileen for the first time in her life needs me. It's an odd feeling to be needed like that. By a kid who's always disliked you.'

'Why does she need you? If she's ill oughtn't she to be looked after by nurses? Isn't it your father's job . . .?'

'It's not his job. At least he knows that. He's run away.'

'What?'

'He's gone to London. On a business trip. Which may keep him for some time. And I believe that if we phoned up her house we'd find that Mrs. Harris has for some reason found she had to go to London, too. It wouldn't surprise me if they went on to Paris. And possibly Rome.'

She laughed suddenly.

'I'm not suggesting that my dear Papa won't respect the decencies. He'll be very fussy about them. After all there's nothing to stop him becoming a public figure now, with that woman's expert help. I hope for his sake he has more stamina than her first.'

'Sarah . . . are you sure it's really like this?'

'Sit down, Ned. It's sweet of you to come. I thought I didn't want to see you, but I do. Drink?'

'Yes, I would like a whisky.'

149

'I'll have one, too.'

I chose the sofa, hoping she would come beside me, but not expecting her to. But she did. She handed me a tumbler and then sat down to tuck her hand under my arm.

'You came as soon as you knew, didn't you, Ned?'

'Sarah, I hadn't a clue. . . .'

'I know, how could you? Don't look so worried, Ned, I'm all right. At first I felt bitter and bottled up and wanting to cry at the same time. But there were other actors with more important parts to play.'

'You mean Eileen and your father?'

'Yes. Eileen had the skids put under her. You see, before she died, my mother told her all about Father and Mrs. Harris.'

I didn't say anything. We both heard that television programme bumbling along in a moronic inaudibility behind us.

'Eileen went all to pieces,' Sarah said. 'She had hysterics after the funeral. I just couldn't have conceived that solid girl going like that unless I'd seen it. We all came back here, bags of relations. And she started, in front of everyone, on my father. Oh, we got her out of the room but not before all the relations were in the picture, if they hadn't been before. It was a good old-fashioned brainstorm, poor kid. The next day she just wept. You know . . . the kind of pity I felt for her was the pity you feel for a suffering animal. It may seem a horrible thing to say, but I can't get away from the idea that all the distress is some way on the surface, that Eileen's not really letting it touch her at all. I don't think it will be long before she solders her world up again to look the way she likes it. Maybe I'm saying this because I'm not really fond of her. Nor she of me. In fact, I think she dislikes me more than ever at the moment.'

'With you doing all this, Sarah?'

'Oh, that's not important. The thing is I remind her of Father in some way. Still, she's decided to claim me as her sister for the time being. She won't have anyone else near her, not yet. But that won't last long. And I've got plans for her cure. I nabbed Father before he went off. You know, he looked old and frightened. He gave me a fat cheque to use as I liked for Eileen and pushed everything into my lap and ran.'

Sarah laughed.

'Ned, I know I've rather shocked you on the matter of parents, haven't I? You've never seen a vestige of the usual polite respect. Quite true. As long as I can remember I've thought they were both fools.'

'And yet you're hurt?'

'I suppose I am. I felt a deep pity for my mother long before I knew anything about this. Very like my feeling for Eileen now. I think I'm probably going to take Eileen away for a time, to Switzerland or France. No use sending her back to school just now. I think a complete change will do the trick. It wouldn't surprise me if Eileen learns to accept her stepmother before I do. And in a way that's a bit hard.'

'I don't get that.'

'Oh, I was thinking of Ma. It was what she was trying to insure against. She told Eileen everything about Father and Mrs. Harris for one reason; because she thought that this way she could get Eileen to refuse to accept her successor. Poor Ma, thinking it all out in her bed. She had no faith in me, that's why I wasn't the one she sent for when she knew she was getting worse. It wouldn't have done any good to tell me. I was too much the neutral in my own family. Eileen seemed her only chance. I've found out that Mother asked the doctor for the truth and he told her. That was when she sent to bring her youngest back from school.'

'I can't see a parent setting out to make her child suffer!'

'Ma had suffered, Ned. And she wasn't used to it. She had no training for the kind of thing that hit at the end of her life. And she was physically helpless, the thing she'd never dreamed she would be. Can't you see? Talking to Eileen was a wild bid for a kind of immortality. She thought she could make Eileen go on blocking the thing she'd tried to block. Poor Ma forgot that Eileen is exactly like her, that pretty soon she'll set about the business of making her life snug again. Just as my mother did, all her days until these last few months when she couldn't.'

Sarah put her head against my shoulder. Her hand tightened on my arm.

'Thank you for saying what you did when you came in, Ned.'

Fourteen

SARAH flew to Switzerland with her sister and she wrote me three times in five weeks. In the second letter Eileen was well enough to climb a minor Alp with a guide. In the third Sarah had sent for her father and James Baillie had gone out from London. The family reunion had been calm. It was as though Sarah had timed it perfectly, knowing exactly the right moment for that meeting. She told me that she thought her father would take Eileen on to Venice, and if that happened she would fly home. It all began to make Ella Baillie seem a long time dead.

At the end of the fifth week Sarah arrived at Turnhouse Airport and I was the only one to meet her. She came down the steps looking brown and healthy, smiling. She kissed me.

'I nearly asked you to come out, Ned.'

'I couldn't have got away.'

'Oh? Busy?'

'Well . . . sort of tidying up.'

'It's getting near that, is it?'

'Pretty near, I guess.'

'You don't know definitely? You're not keeping anything from me?'

'No, Sarah.'

She got into my car and slammed the door.

'Are you going back to live alone in that house?' I asked.

'No, my father's cousin is coming to stay. She ought to be there now. I told the old man that I was going to have to work like mad to catch up on my part and that I simply couldn't function as a temporary housekeeper. So he whistled up a poor relation. He'd do anything for me just now. It gives me such an odd feeling of power.'

As I drove I asked:

'How's Eileen?'

'Blooming. She's chilly to Pa, but she tolerates him. A bit more actually. And she wanted to go to Venice because it's *en fête* with some kind of film festival.'

'You're not worried about her any more?'

'Not in the slightest. Nor Pa, if I ever was. I read him a little lecture and told him he wasn't to marry Mrs. Harris for one year. I also told him that when he did we would all rally round and keep up the family front.'

I didn't say anything to that. In one year Sarah planned still to be in Edinburgh. I knew there was no chance I would be.

'Angus is a bit fraught about your part, Sarah. I saw him a couple of nights ago. He said that if you didn't show up in another week he would have to get someone else.'

'Well, I'm here. And anyway, he'd no intention of getting anyone else. Sweetie, I'm not going to be seeing much of you. I've got to sweat, you know that?'

'I know that, Sarah.'

'Do you mind frightfully? Is this play just a lot of nonsense to you?'

'If it isn't to you, how could it be to me?'

Sarah laughed.

'I don't think I really like you when you're being humble like that. It's a patent fraud.'

'Okay. I hate the play like hell. I'd like to go to Paris with you for a gay week-end.'

'I'm very, very tired of abroad,' Sarah said. 'I dislike foreigners, and hotels, and the sun all the time, and the cooking. Also, wherever I go that delightful little local vintage always seems a bit sour, and it upsets my stomach. I have to go

about with an eye open for suitable female conveniences, and
they're terribly scarce. If you want a wild week-end we'll go up
to Pitlochry.'

'Isn't that where the salmon jump up a ladder?'

'That's right. And there's also a summer theatre. Doing
adaptations of the Scots classics.'

'I might have guessed,' I said.

The Baillie door in Morningside was opened by a woman in
her sixties who looked as though she had spent a considerable
portion of her life travelling to other people's domestic crises.

'Well, Sarah,' she said.

Sarah went up and kissed her. Sarah asked whether everything had been all right, whether she'd found the boiler in and
something to eat. Then I was introduced.

Miss Emmeline McKay had a touch of colour in her cheeks
now. She looked at Sarah as though, long ago, against the
judgment of many, she had decided to like this child. And I
was suddenly conscious in that meeting that I'd never seen
Sarah patronize anyone. She had described this woman as a
poor relation, that was a fact. It was also a fact that there was
no suggestion of this in the way Sarah treated her.

'I have tea ready for you both, dear.'

'Emmy, can I be a beast and run upstairs and have a bath
and change? I want to get out of the clothes I've travelled in.
Don't wait for me, you give Ned his tea.'

Miss McKay and I went into the drawing-room and I was
given my tea. We talked about the weather and that it was soon
going to be the Festival again and what was I going to see?
I told about my mother coming to Scotland and that caught her
interest.

'Oh. She's coming over just now? I see. I wonder . . . I
mean, are you Sarah's intended?'

'Am I . . .? Oh. Well . . . I'm not certain.'

Miss McKay smiled.

'I didn't mean to pry. Dear Sarah, I'm very fond of her.'

Again there was that hint of this opinion not travelling right
alongside the general family one. She sipped her tea, looked at

the fire and then told me how sorry she was not to have been able to get up to Ella Baillie's funeral, but she had been busy nursing another relation down with jaundice in Dumfries. I rather gathered from this that she had missed the sensation, and echoes of it hadn't reached her yet.

'She was true blue,' Miss McKay said suddenly.

My eyebrows must have shot up.

'I mean dear Ella. I always thought her such a straight person. You always knew exactly where you were with her. A spade was a spade, you see.'

My silence must have seemed encouraging.

'I knew her right from the time she married James. They were in Lanark first, you know. Such a funny little house. And then they moved to Edinburgh, to a semi-detached at Liberton. I remember thinking that was very grand, and so did Ella. It was from Liberton that she took up golf.'

'Oh, yes.'

'I don't think that in her heart Ella wanted to leave Liberton, you know. It was a perfectly good house, it had four bedrooms and a garage. But, of course, by that time James was getting on. I mean, he had a position to keep up, I suppose. This house has always struck me as rather chilly.'

'It can be cold in winter.'

Miss McKay smiled.

'You've noticed that? I always think of Liberton as the family house. I mean the family was growing up, Eileen a baby, and Sarah at school. It was all so different. James was . . . well, rather a jolly man in those days. You know, I've been looking at an album. When I saw Ella after she first had to go to bed, she had it in her room. We looked at it together. I wondered if it would still be there and it was. I brought it down here. Do you think Sarah will mind?'

'I shouldn't think so for one moment, Miss McKay.'

'One never knows with young people. But perhaps you would be interested in seeing Sarah at the age of three?'

My interest could have been kept under control, but she wanted to look at pictures, and so we sat side by side on the sofa and looked at them, turning over the heavy black pages from which the white prints glared out.

'There she is! Isn't she sweet? That's Sarah!'

She wasn't sweet really, just a little girl, rather too plump, with chubby legs and a most extraordinary hair-do.

'That's Ella.'

I'd have known her all right, not quite so heavy about the head, but still a generously sized woman, in a longish skirt, holding up something, a silver cup, with other women holding clubs grouped behind her. It must have been the Liberton phase when the golf started.

There were more of Ella over the pages, all of them out of doors, one standing by the new family saloon, the general impression of the lost years coming over as a kind of elongated picnic. There was even James, standing in the sea, splashing his wife.

'Emmy! What on earth's that?'

We hadn't heard Sarah come in. She had changed and caught her hair back from her face with two clips in a way I hadn't seen before.

'Oh, Sarah. It's your mother's album. I was showing it. . . . You don't mind, do you?'

'No. Of course not. But . . . where did you get it? In Mother's room?'

'Yes, I'll put it back.'

'No . . . don't! That is . . . Emmy, would you like it?'

'I would, but . . . there's you and your father? And Eileen. It's a family record, dear.'

'You keep the records of our family, Emmy.'

'Do you really mean that? You're sure?'

'Quite sure.' Sarah touched the teapot. 'This seems cold. I'll make fresh.'

Sarah and I never got to Pitlochry . . . there wasn't even time to look at a fish ladder. Once we drove down to the golf resort of Gullane and had very good food in a place that reminded me of a New England country eating-house, antiques, spinning-wheel and the general tone of discreet emphasis on the things it takes money to buy. Another day we travelled a hundred miles to see Loch Lomond, which looked dark to me, and on the way back stopped for dinner at one of Scotland's glossy pubs, where the oak in the Rob Roy bar was carefully decayed to that point where it would just continue to hold together for American tourists. The dining-room was full of American tourists eating tinned corn on the cob at one dollar twenty cents a cob. While we were there eight Rolls Royces packed with Americans from a super cruise ship at Oban drew up, and the hotel lobby seemed to me suddenly filled with the very loud noise of people whose experience of living had taught them that you could buy it.

Sarah kept watching me.

'Makes you feel like an established native, doesn't it, Ned?'

'In a way. But more in a limbo.'

'Right out on your own?'

'Kind of.'

'Oh, sweetie! Why don't you take out Scots naturalization papers? My pa would think you were just the type for the building trade. You're young, personable and a hustler.'

'Go on . . . damn me.'

'Wouldn't you like a nice house in one of Edinburgh's restricted suburbs? All American comforts. Oil central heating, automatic refuse disposer, master bedroom with its own bath. We can offer all these comforts now. Pa puts up houses like that all the time.'

'The minimum standard for the civilized life. Plus an actress wife?'

'Ned, I'd rather set out to be cosy with you than anyone else. You know I can begin to see it, me making little excursions from our secure background. The right part in the right play once every two years. Plus appearances in a television panel game.'

'You're not really seeing it.'

She laughed.

'But I know I ought to. Any natural woman of my age is

thinking about a nest for the little ones. Can you see me a doting mother?'

'I can see you a sensible one.'

'But that's not the same!'

'I believe it's much better all round.'

'What . . . no cocoon of love?'

'Give them affection, give them your interest, but take damn' good care to see that life kicks them on the backside every now and then. It's going to do it anyway. They might as well get the feel early. You could say it was kindest.'

'Ned! You're beginning to sound like one of our fathers of the military classes.'

'I tell you, I'm getting corrupted. I'm not even sure I believe in the American home any more. And if they ever suspect that, I'll be purged.'

Sarah sat back and laughed.

'You're just sour. Too many of your own countrymen at adjoining tables. I know the feeling. I had it in Switzerland.'

I opened my case and held it across the table.

'You're even smoking our cigarettes,' she said. 'But you weren't really thinking about that house in our suburb, were you?'

'No.'

'It's where you go she goes, too?'

'Uh-huh.'

'Palembang or to hell with you? I think you're probably right.'

In the car again, driving over the bouncing, pretty country towards Stirling, I asked Sarah if she would marry me and come to Palembang. She said she would think about it. I asked her where she was going to live when she left the Morningside mansion and she said probably Glasgow. I told her that the climate was almost certainly nicer in Palembang, that it got the winds off the Indian Ocean, that we could have a house up behind the town. I also pointed out that if she was afraid of things getting dull, there was a very good chance of being caught up in a revolution, that Sumatra was as yet far from quiet, and we might even be in at the birth of a democracy. She said that she thought seventy-two miles an hour was too fast for a road with as many bends in it as the one we were on, and Angus would be upset if she had to miss any more rehearsals through hospitalization.

The road began to straighten out as we went past Kippen where they have the biggest grapevine in Scotland. The car reached seventy-eight and stayed there, quiet and happy with it. We didn't say much. I was thinking that it was the damnedest thing to have worked yourself slowly and somewhat painfully into love and to feel the pincers of it biting into you.

Fifteen

MAMA arrived three days before the Festival opened in Edinburgh. This was because something had happened down in Italy to her schedule. She sent me a long telegram about that which had been translated from Italian into English. That telegram was a pretty good argument for the view still held by some that there are certain difficulties to be overcome before anyone can establish a United States of Europe. But I did get the train time and was down in Waverley Station to meet the express which steamed in twenty minutes late.

I'd had a trying day. It isn't easy just before the Festival opens to persuade Edinburgh hotel-keepers to alter long-standing reservations. In fact, in the end, I'd failed and I'd had to squeeze my family party into a hotel on the outskirts of the city which I knew Mama wasn't going to like one little bit. There's always a shortage of bathrooms in British hotels by American standards, but this one out near the country offered an acute shortage. Mama was going to have to walk down a flight of stairs and along a passage and into another passage and up three steps and there it was, with a boxed-in zinc tub and all. I hadn't dared make any enquiries about the food, but there was certainly a smell of it when you got through the front door.

I could feel the palms of my hands sticky as that express came rumbling to a stop. I'd chosen what I thought was a strategic spot, just opposite the place where a porter had told me the first-class carriages stopped. The thing that drew up by me was the dining-car and on both sides of it were second-class carriages. It was the longest train I think I'd ever seen and suddenly the whole platform was filled with 'cellos and people shouting in foreign languages, with the men using their hands in a very un-British way, and quite pretty girls, who might be out of a chorus line in some ballet, looking up at the grimed roof of the station and squeaking. There were also a lot of those baggage trolleys being propelled at terrific speed by little men who grinned and aimed at you.

I went as fast as I could in an easterly direction, but of course I was too late. Mama was off the train and saw me first. She was advancing, followed by a porter trying to carry a lot of those light-coloured wardrobe suitcases that look nice in Macy's window but take a terrible beating in Europe. She was carrying a lot of things herself, but she managed to stretch out her arms in a gesture that was for me and the world.

'Junior!'

I think I may have winced. I've never been Junior outside of Abilene.

'Junior! My boy!'

Suddenly I was glad to see her. I hadn't often played a leading role in my family and this was a moment for me. I kissed her on a carefully shaped mouth and then on both cheeks. She smelled of Chanel No. 5 and chain-smoking.

'Junior! Let me look at you. Why you haven't changed one little bit. You've still got that silly hair-cut. I didn't think the barbers over here would do it that way. You look like a college boy, do you know that?'

'I don't feel like any college boy, Mama.'

'Oh! Oh, it's wonderful. Here I am in Edinburgh at last. In Scotland. And you're meeting me! It's been a kind of dream, Junior. Where's Louise? I thought she was coming right along behind. Where *is* Louise? Here, porter, don't go running off. We got to find my daughter. It's that boy. He's the nicest boy, but I don't think they *see* anything. We met up with him again in Paris. He wasn't coming to Scotland, but Louise just said he had to come. You know, Junior, this boy is very nice. He's got a real brain.'

I'd gambled on the fella not coming, and lost. There was no hotel accommodation for him and no tickets. And then I saw Louise and the boy with the real brain. They were carrying nothing. Louise was looking at him. He had the Yul Brunner hair treatment, which made me decide to grow mine much longer, and Louise must have been got at by one of those French stylists. I remembered her as a kid with a mop of brown hair but now it had all been cut off except for chunks, and the chunks stuck out all over, and they hung down over her forehead. Her lips were cerise and from four yards the mascara almost hid her eyes.

But she could still see. I was spotted, suddenly.

'Junior! O-o-oh!'

That was drawn out like a banshee wail. When she hit me I was almost moved back from the impact. I found, to my astonishment, that she was weeping in my arms. I couldn't quite place myself in the emotional scene, and Louise really didn't do anything to help, she just hung on.

'You're right here!' she said a few times, as though I'd been something in her mind for long enough, a thing I couldn't believe.

'Now don't let's get silly,' Mama said. 'You'll have Junior crying right here on the platform.'

I met Yul, whose name was Tommy. That is, he was indicated and I said 'hello' and he made a kind of cryptic lodge sign with one hand, his lips never moving.

You could see that Tommy was burdened by his brain, his face rigid with the responsibility for it. He was a sophomore at Cornell and came from Massachusetts which made him almost as mysterious for Louise as a Frenchman.

Mama liked my car. It was exactly like the one friends of hers in Abilene had traded in two years ago, but she'd liked the old one better. We drove up the ramp out of the station and into Princes Street, with Mama talking about Italy and how

163

hot it had been, a different kind of heat from Texas, but hot. In the back seat Louise and Tommy weren't saying anything. I could see him in the driving mirror, not looking out at all, apparently staring at the back of my head.

They didn't notice at first when I turned towards the country, but soon it was apparent that this was no longer the city centre. Mama asked about that and I explained.

'Junior! Do you mean to say you haven't got us fixed up in the right hotel?'

'Mama, it's the Festival!'

'But you're right here! Why, I never even thought for a moment it would be much trouble. Why, Junior, we can't live way out here!'

'Mama, you'll get into your hotel when the Festival starts.'

'Do you mean to say we've got to live right out here in the country? We didn't come to Scotland to live right out in the country, Junior.'

'Mama, I've done my best, I promise you that. There isn't a room in this town in the big hotels. It's packed tight.'

'Well!'

It was a nice evening—soft light from the Pentland Hills, lemon-tinted clouds with rose behind them. But that hotel I'd found still looked awful.

'Don't get out the bags,' Mama said, when we stopped.

I went in with her. She was completely charming. She approached the depressed-looking proprietor with all the caution of someone dealing for the first time with Zulus.

'I'd just like to see your accommodation. Do you mind?'

She went and saw it while I waited. And then she came down the stairs chatting. She said that the bedroom she had just inspected had a wonderful view. She thanked the proprietor. She was sure there were a lot of people who would want that room.

On the steps she said to me:

'We'll go back into town. To that hotel where I have my reservations.'

There was no use trying to tell her that I'd spent a total of about six hours waiting near the reception desk of that down-town hotel for sudden cancellations. I just drove them all back into town and on this trip the front seat was as silent as the back. At the hotel Mama got out. I said I couldn't park the car, I'd have to stay in case the police came. Mama went through the revolving doors.

In just seven minutes by the dashboard clock she was out again, coming across the pavement to us, smiling. She was followed by a hotel porter in uniform.

'It's all right,' she called out. 'There's been a cancellation. And there's a little room for Tommy on the top floor.'

I had dinner with them in the crowded restaurant. There was no trouble about that, the waiter was attentive, the food elaborately adequate, and after the meal Louise and Tommy went out to see the latest picture of a male actor in the business for twenty-five years who'd just had his face lifted. Mama and I went and sat in the lounge, in a window looking out on the Castle where they were trying out the flood-lighting.

'It's just beautiful, Junior. It's like a dream. Are you smoking British cigarettes?'

'Yes.'

'Well, they should be tipped. Our doctor says there's a certain protection in tipped cigarettes. I tell everyone that. Everyone we know is smoking tipped cigarettes.'

'Would you like a drink, Mama?'

'Oh, no. Are you drinking a lot, Junior?'

'No. It's just that after a meal . . .'

'I don't know why you would need it after a meal. I can understand *before* all right. Do you know you're thinner?'

'My weight's been the same for the last five years.'

'Oh, no. I can *see* you're thinner, Junior. You haven't got a cough?'

I'd just been going to. It got held.

'Junior, is there something troubling you? I've felt it ever since I got off that train. And before, too. From the letters. They weren't the same. Something had gone out of them. It's been worrying me, it's been worrying me a lot. Junior . . . is it a girl?'

'Aren't you rushing things a bit, Mama?'

'Why is it rushing things to ask your son if he's got a girl? Sometimes I've had the feeling that you want to cut yourself off from the rest of us. That you don't want to tell us things. Oh, don't protest! You know what I mean, in your heart, if you look there. Why should this be, Junior? We're your family, we're your people. My feeling is you don't give us a chance any more.'

'Mama, I live all over the world.'

'You could try to come home more often. Don't tell me you couldn't do it in these days of planes. I know you get a big salary, and you could afford it. Are you saving your money to get married to this girl, is that it?'

'I don't think the girl is going to marry me!'

'Oh. Are you not good enough for her? Is she British?'

'Yes.'

'Is she Scotch? Does she live right here in Edinburgh?'

'Yes.'

'And you've been hurt bad?'

'Mama, please. . . .'

'Junior, don't try to squirm out of things. You always used to try and squirm out of things when you were a little boy. Oh, you were honest. I'm not saying you weren't. But you'd twist away, sometimes, like you're doing now.'

'I'm not twisting out of anything!'

'But you are, you know. And it upsets me. It upsets me, too, to find that my son isn't good enough for a Scotch girl. Have you been making a fool of yourself, Junior?'

'Possibly!'

'I'm sorry to hear that. I'm terribly, terribly sorry to hear it.'

'Mama, can we drop this?'

'If you want to. I'm not going to meet this girl, I suppose?'

'If you want to, you can. I'm sure she'd be willing . . . I know she'd like to meet you.'

'You don't sound terribly convinced. Is that because you

don't think this girl is interested enough in you to be interested in your mother?'

'I . . . she's got a career. She's working very hard at the moment.'

'Why specially at the moment, Junior?'

'Because she's an actress!'

'Oh!'

'Her father's a big man in the building trade. He owns a lot of property here. Sarah went to London but she's back again.'

My mother was watching me. I was disgusted with myself for having rushed to put Sarah into a financially stable background.

'Is she a good actress, Junior?'

'I . . . I haven't seen her on the stage. Only in radio work.'

'I don't mind what people do so long as they do it with their whole heart. That's what our minister always says back home. It's not what you do, it's the spirit you put into it, Junior.'

'Yes, Mama.'

'This girl wasn't such a success down in London?'

'She . . .'

I glared at the flood-lit Castle and clamped my mouth shut. My mother turned her head and looked out, too.

'They seem to be dancing down there,' she said. 'Isn't that cute, dancing in the open air? I'd have thought it was too cold over here. Have you got used to the climate?'

'I guess I have in a way.'

'Could you live in Scotland? I mean so that it would feel like home?'

'I have been living here and in a way it has felt like home.'

'Oh! Junior, how about us going out for a little in your car? There's still some light. I want you to tell me all about that ancestor of our family out on his island.'

'But I wrote it all to you in Italy.'

'I know, but I want to hear it again.'

We got into my car and I decided to take my mother out on to the Braid Hills drive and let her see the lights coming on and the glowing Castle against the distant hills of Fife. It was the kind of dramatic view that gave Americans the feeling of getting their money's worth, and it was a clear night.

I turned on the radio to Germany and got an American announcing one of those rather rare hours of potpourri classical music. Each item was explained to us by a metallic voice which certainly belonged to an egghead serving time in the army. We were two Americans riding around in an American car listening to an American voice in the intervals between music on tape. My mother was smoking one of her tipped cigarettes.

'This is nice, Junior. You know, I just knew I was going to like it as soon as I got settled in that hotel. I knew I was going to feel at home in Scotland.'

I arranged the meeting between my mother and Sarah in a cocktail bar. It is more difficult for any one person to dominate a situation where everyone is standing up. Louise and Tommy were there, too, Louise watching him all the time as though expecting he might say something suddenly which would open another oyster of experience. But Tommy didn't; he just looked exhausted after a day of silent sightseeing.

Mama's feet hurt, and she was a little surprised that she got her whisky on ice just the way she liked it back home. She always had one with father in the evening when he came back from the office. I'd sometimes suspected that my father stopped off on the way home for a few to help that one out, but I'd never caught him at it, only noticed the cheerfulness which lasted until he had food in his stomach.

'My, I'm so excited,' Mama said. 'I mean it's worked out all to the good, coming early. We're going to see the real opening of the Festival. I'm just sorry, Ned, that you didn't get us seats in the cathedral to see the religious ceremony. That would have been quite an experience.'

'You can watch the procession from the square, Mama.'

'If it means more standing I just don't think I can take it. You know my arches nearly fell once? That was a terrible time. I had to do special exercises for a year.'

'Would you like to sit down now? I'll get you a stool.'

'Oh, no, not if the rest of you are standing. Do you like this place, Ned? Do you come here a lot? I was just noticing the ventilation doesn't seem to be terribly good. You'd think they'd have conditioning.'

My mother was very carefully dressed. She had gone back to the hotel to change and she was in black, packed into it; her figure allowed no concessions to time. She'd had her hair done that morning, not the way she liked it, but better than in Italy. She hadn't thought much of the hairdressers in Italy.

She was ready for the occasion, alert, her eyes always ready to flick to the door. I was more nervous than I'd felt for years. What I was doing was a kind of cruelty, and I knew it. There was never much excuse for a meeting arranged like this, under compulsion, an inspection on the one side, and a defence against it on the other.

Sarah had agreed at once, as though it was an obligation, when it wasn't. I had no claim on her which justified any ordeals, and I was conscious then of this visit turning out as the thing I had dreaded, a renewal of the child-parent relationship with no real concessions on my mother's part to change.

It can't ever be easy for parents to accept their children as adults; the inevitable long history of dependence works against this; but you do sometimes see an effort towards adjustment made, sincere on both sides, and something new can emerge. I knew it never could between Mother and me. I was Junior and that was that. It was assumed that I must be continuously in her debt, first because she was my mother—a state with a flavour of holiness about it—and secondly because her existence in time would always remain twenty-seven years in advance of mine.

I sipped whisky and toyed with heresy. Could one, after all, love to specifications? Could feeling come from duty, from a mystical bond of blood patterns? Perhaps it wasn't so strange that the Chinese, who had worshipped filial piety for four thousand years, should have been able to switch almost overnight to a worship of the converse. A society with a papa or mama idolatry may well be carrying the seeds of its sudden destruction there.

It wasn't possible, either, to pity my mother. She was too highly organized. She set the limits of the world she wanted and moved through it in triumph.

'Your friend's late,' Mama said.

'She may have been kept at rehearsal.'

But that wasn't why Sarah was late. I saw her in the doorway and knew she had gone home to change. Like my mother she was wearing black, a safe colour for the uncertain occasion, instinctive to many women. But Sarah had made the mistake of using too much make-up with it, and the result was a strained sophistication, almost a hardness, which I had seen before.

James Baillie was with his daughter. It was the first time I had seen him since his wife's death and he looked, beside Sarah in very high heels, almost a small man, and now oddly diminished in his own importance. It was as though the hustler had been forced to stop and hadn't quite got started again. Father and daughter came into the room together, both smiling, and the stranger mightn't have seen the uneasiness behind those smiles.

The introductions were my mother's cue. She emerged from them with the initiative in talk and I knew she wasn't going to let it go. Sarah was pecked at with a synthetic warmth. You sensed at once a basic antipathy between these two that nothing could ever change, already setting hard behind the smiles and the words.

'My dear Sarah, I was just saying to Ned today that all this is quite an experience for us. I mean to come to Edinburgh just now and meet up with a participant in the Festival! It's not a thing we expected at all. How could we? We're just tourists. And we hadn't realized how deeply Ned had got tied up with living over here.'

Mr. Baillie was working harder than his daughter. He asked Tommy if he had seen Edinburgh University and the brain reacted to that, suddenly, almost an explosion.

'Yeh!' Tommy paused. 'That old stone certainly holds the dirt.'

It was more than I'd ever got out of the boy, but I don't think Mr. Baillie quite appreciated his triumph. Only Louise was goggle-eyed. If she'd had a notebook handy she'd have used it. The prestige of the East Coast intellectual certainly hangs on in the States whatever we may say about it out where there's more sky.

'Now listen,' Mama said. 'This isn't really any place for us to get to know each other. Why don't we all go back to my hotel and have dinner? Mr. Baillie, are you free tonight?'

'Sarah can scarcely be free just now, Mother,' I said.

Sarah looked at me.

'But I am free, you know. We've the dress rehearsal to-morrow. Nothing before that.'

I might have known Sarah would take a deep breath and plunge in.

'Well, then,' said Mama. 'Isn't that just fine? Ned, I suggest that you go and phone the hotel right now. And tell them to give us a table for six. A round table.'

'A what?'

'A round table, Ned. I like sitting the way you can see everyone.'

'Mama, the place is packed out.'

My mother smiled at me.

'I know. And you're the one who said I couldn't get a room, let alone a room for Tommy. Just give them my name and ask for a *round* table. If you don't want to do it, I'll do it myself.'

'I'll do it!'

'That boy . . .' I heard her say as I went out of the cocktail bar.

When I got back Mother had got hold of Mr. Baillie's first name and was waving it around.

'Jamie! Isn't that the cutest thing? All our James become Jim, but Jamie is just enchanting. You know, Jamie, I'm going to remember that and when some of my friends have a baby

I'm going to tell them to call him Jamie, that it's the real Scotch way to do. You know, we've got an awful lot of Scotch people out our way, you'd be surprised. In Dallas there's a party they have every year and some of the men wear the kilts.'

'Kilt, Mama.'

'What?'

'It's singular.'

'Oh, but I mean a lot of them.'

'It's still singular.'

'Well, isn't that odd? I don't believe Ned knows anyway. Do you think he knows, Sarah?'

'He's turned out a quick learner,' Sarah said.

And Mother looked from me to her and then back to me again.

On the pavement outside I caught hold of Sarah's arm and held her back.

'How's it going, honey?'

'You mean this or the play?'

'We won't talk about this. You let yourself in for the round table. I meant the play.'

'It's hell.'

'I don't believe it.'

'Ned, I was glad to come tonight. To have something else to think about. Angus is nearly out of his head. And I don't blame him. I'm . . .'

I stopped her.

'Sarah, what is it?'

'I'm . . . terrible.'

'I don't believe it.'

'Oh . . . you would! I can't seem to get it. Edna just plays circles round me. And it's a gift. My part, I mean. To the right actress. I'm like wood.'

'Sarah, I love you and I don't believe it! Do you hear? You can't do this to yourself! It isn't in you to do it. On the night you'll . . .'

'On the night! Ned, I can't think about it, I tell you. I lay last night and I couldn't sleep. I'm hollow.'

'Sarah, remember on Gigha, on that beach? What you said about help? Lawrence's fine chisel and the blows that weren't your own blows? You believed it could happen. You said it had.'

'Oh, it can happen. But why should it? Ned, I haven't earned anything. I feel I haven't earned a damn' thing. Come on, they're looking back at us, we've got to go!'

Sixteen

THE Edinburgh Festival is almost treated as an occasion by the critics. Every London paper and journal of repute sends up its big names, including the two solemn Sundays. Some of the critics even stay the whole three weeks, and the coverage is pretty adequate, if a shade patronizing. It's about the only event in the British calendar year in which London notices anything outside its own limits.

The official dramatic offerings this time were yet another serio-comic by Mr. Eliot, a week devoted to a Queen of the French theatre offering a re-heat of the mouldiest classic corn in her repertoire, and—in the Assembly Hall of the Church of Scotland with its penitential wooden pews—a vast spectacle written by a Welsh schoolmaster as yet unknown, with a cast of eighty-seven, plus commissioned music.

All this made the promoters of unofficial Fringe productions pretty optimistic. Many of the critics would have their reactions to Mr. Eliot written before they left home, those who liked the French Queens would go on liking them, and everyone was certain to jump on the Welsh schoolmaster almost at once. This would leave the *gauleiters* of English criticism with their work done and a lot of time on their hands after the first week. Since a number of these were either conscientious, or bored with the Festival Club, there was a very good chance that most of the Fringe productions would be seen and even commented on.

Angus had, I thought, been very shrewd indeed. Mr. Maxwell Anderson was well known even in England as one of the fathers of American drama, and the established celebrity always gets the benefit of any doubt there may be. Also, the production had money spent on it, good baker's money, and was meant to be an eye-as well as an earful, well worth the price of a seat as a spectacle alone. If it should, as Angus had hoped, turn out to be more than a spectacle in his version, he would have struck a real blow for his own prestige as a character of some standing beyond the borders of the little country which had, up to now, contained him.

Mary of Scotland opened on a Tuesday. On the Monday I met Angus in the packed bar of the Festival Club, a surprise this, because I had thought you must sit with the baby all the time at this stage. He spotted me, but gave no sign, and when I went up, and he looked at me, I felt the first pang of sympathy for him I had ever experienced.

His pounded face was puffy. In his eyes was the stifled agony of a wounded animal which isn't going to make a fuss about dying. He could have been watching, over a stretched-out misery of weeks, the gradual withering of his hopes. There was a kind of frightful dignity about Angus then, Angus a little drunk, standing back against the wall of a bar.

An opening gambit wasn't going to be easy. I saw he was drinking his usual and went away and got him another.

'Thanks,' he said, taking it, and handing me an empty glass. 'Well, well, Ned. Having a look at your second Festival, is that it? Thinking that twice is enough, perhaps?'

'I'm being a kind of Cook's guide to relations. I'm meeting them here for lunch.'

'But you're not involved, son. You're not a God-damned fool!'

'Angus!'

'The profanity upsets you? My apologies. I usually avoid it, too. A kind of caution from Presbyterian ancestors. There may, after all, be the recorder with the indelible pencil.'

'Angus, is it so bloody?'

'You have chosen the word well. Have you been seeing Sarah?'

'No. She doesn't seem to be seeing anyone right now.'

'I'm not surprised.'

'Angus, you can't blame Sarah!'

'I'm not blaming Sarah. She's only part of it. You wouldn't understand. I don't think you could come near it. I can imagine how you sum all this up. Angus the showman, and this was my circus. Well, damn it, it wasn't! Not altogether. In fact not much when I got started. This is a play, Ned. It has shape and form and moments that could get you in the guts. It's not going to get anyone in the guts. And that's not the author's fault, it's mine. I'm the provincial grey-haired boy who isn't going to shake 'em. If you'll excuse me I'll buy myself another drink.'

'Angus, come out of this place and eat something.'

'I thought you were meeting relatives?'

'I'll leave a message for them.'

'Hell, why should you?'

'I happen to want to.'

We went to a fish restaurant I'd found down Leith Walk. All the regular places would be seething. We got a booth and had fried fillet of sole.

'Go on, eat it,' I said.

'I ought to appreciate this traditional act, Ned. I don't know that I do. I've never thought of you as a friend of mine. Are you a friend of mine?'

'I haven't been doing any analysis.'

He laughed.

'The moment of weakness gets you. You couldn't stand the man who knew where he was going.'

'You're probably right. Eat your fish.'

Angus was right in a way; the moment of weakness had got me. But there was more than that to it, something I'd identified before in him, call it the artist, that drive to create in imagination which did transcend his social personality. And it was the artist that had taken the beating, the thing he wanted to make turned to dust. He was sick in spirit and it was sad to see.

'Angus, are you rehearsing this afternoon?'

'No, no, no. Tonight.'

'Then will you listen to me? Go home and take a sedative and sleep for three hours.'

He smiled.

'Good sound advice, Ned, good sound advice. Will you run me in your car?'

He swayed a little on the stairs up to his flat. His voice echoed in the high, converted hall of the huge house as he stood half-way up a flight, looking back at me.

'You've got a very nice line with people in a neurotic state, Ned. I've got to hand it to you there. And it wasn't something I'd looked for. The gentleness. But I suppose it fits in with the research work, the peering at us. Haven't you been peering? Gathering data? You reminded me of all those boys from your country with Ph.D.s who are competing so effectively with the Germans. Usually they work on the dead, of course. But I can see you producing something long enough on us to be authoritative. Isn't that the word? Pages and pages and pages and on every page three footnotes. One, two, three. Smaller print. Get it?'

'The fish hasn't quite dealt with the alcohol. But I think I get it.'

'Hm. Not in the least irritated, are you? Calm and cool. The oil man who might have been a school teacher. I've been a fool. You're always a fool to gamble on things happening with other people that you can use. I gambled on using Sarah in love. See?'

'I'd rather you dropped this line, Angus.'

'Oh, but I'm not going to. Hit a drunk if you like! Sarah in love. Sarah able to feel for that Queen we had from France who found the man she wanted too late. Sarah in love! It was the only thing that would have made her come alive in this play.

177

She hasn't got the reserves of feeling to draw on, she has to use what's happening to her now. Maybe that's because she's young, because it takes time to build up the reserves. I don't know. All I know is she hasn't got them. Oh, don't think I'm blaming her for everything. But she's a kind of key, and it isn't turning in the lock. And do you know why that key isn't turning? Because she had to pick a Yank with a nice hygienic hair-cut for her experience.'

'Damn you, I'll . . .!'

'Go on! Hit a drunk. I'll fall relaxed. It won't do me much damage.'

'Angus, you're going to listen to me!'

'Delighted, old boy.'

'I wasn't doing Red Cross work today. I'm not quite so thick that I couldn't see how much you didn't want me around. But I had something to say to you, and that's why I stayed.'

Angus began to laugh. He clutched on to the railings with both hands and sagged over them, laughing.

'Splendid. You've found the solution to me? And to think I gave up the hunt twenty-five years ago.'

'I don't care a damn about you. But you can do something.'

'Pardon, as the Duchess said to the Butler?'

'I said you can do something. I've seen you at it. In an empty studio with a lot of bored actors not expecting anything to happen. You made something happen. Maybe what I saw was just a routine rehearsal to you. And not very important. But you weren't going over lines, you were fighting to make them come alive. And they did in a kind of way. I've never had much feeling for the theatre but I could see it. You were making something out of a radio serial for which you expected a bottom-of-the-poll listener return.'

He had turned right around on the step, staring.

'Are you telling me . . .?'

'I think there's still a chance you can do it with this play. Whatever you may think right now.'

He got the railings again and began to pull himself up.

'I'm feeling . . . that I ought to be in bed.'

'Don't take that sedative until you've lost the fried fish.'

From the landing he looked down at me. Then he swung away, fumbling for his key.

Edinburgh has a lot of temporary theatres during the Festival, gymnasiums and Masonic meeting places, but Angus had got hold of one of the best of these, the hall of some kind of welfare settlement which had an almost full-sized stage and tip-up seats that could take five hundred people. There was even the feel of a British theatre about it, people smoking and being heavily bright before the lights went down and hid them. No one was very well dressed, as though it was silly to dress up just to sit in the dark.

My mother, however, had come straight from an early meal at her hotel, wearing a dinner dress. We were in our seats ten minutes before the curtain, and she found plenty of time to look around.

'Junior, I must admit I'm disappointed in one thing. The Festival isn't chic. At the opening concert most of the women looked as though they were trying to ward off pneumonia.'

'Maybe they were, Mama.'

'Well, I don't think it's good enough. This is after all supposed to be an international cultural occasion. But the Edinburgh Festival dresses exactly like Tourist Class on the *Queen Elizabeth*.'

Somewhere just beyond the horrible vacuum inside of me I could appreciate that.

'I'm glad you believe in complimenting the man you're out with, Mama.'

'I got this dress in Rome, Junior. It didn't seem too young for me there, but after a few days in this city I'm starting to feel that a woman of my years ought to be wearing lilac. And a boa.'

'Think of what you'll be able to do with that Rome dress back home.'

'Why? You can buy exclusive Diors in Dallas. It's something I'm always pointing out to your father. He says he doesn't see why American clothes aren't good enough for American women. Your father always believes in everything American. I think that's because one side of his family was Lithuanian German with a name like Hamburger. He doesn't like to be reminded of it. He's a citizen of the States and doesn't look to Europe. It might embarrass him.'

'You're sharp tonight, Mama.'

'Don't you think I usually am? Don't you think I know you're in a cold sweat?'

That startled me. I didn't think it showed.

'The moment I saw you tonight, Junior, I was reminded of something. You may have forgotten. You were going around with a crowd that included that Renfrew girl. You were seventeen. You knew what I thought of her and what everyone thought of her. And so you went on and dated her alone. Something happened on that date which shouldn't have. You came back from it looking like you do right at this minute.'

'And you said nothing at all?'

'That's right, Junior. I said nothing at all. There are times when it isn't easy for a mother to do that. But I made myself. I had a feeling that you wouldn't date that Renfrew girl again, and you never did. You'd learned your lesson. I think you'll probably never make the same mistake twice.'

'That's reassuring.'

'You think you can run away from me, don't you Junior? You think you can shut doors and be safe on the other side? But you're my son, and I know you. I know what's fine in you and what isn't. And like every mother I hope that what is fine is going to be the thing that endures.'

I whispered.

'It seems to me that Louise on the other side of you has got big ears turned this way.'

'Louise has not got big ears. She's got MacDonald ears. And anyway, she's not listening. Isn't this show late in starting?'

'A minute or two. After all, it's their first night.'

'I've never seen a play by Maxwell Anderson. It's a funny

thing that I've got to come all the way to Scotland to see a play by an American.'

'You wouldn't have had to come to Scotland to do that if you'd lived in New York.'

'So you're beginning to think everything Eastern is wonderful, are you? Well let me tell you something, Ned, they're building right now the biggest theatrical centre in the world in Dallas. And there's going to be a drama school and everything.'

'That'll give you a chance to see more Maxwell Anderson.'

Just then the lights went out.

I'd never before sat in a theatre and watched a play in which every word was familiar to me, some of the words with a power to stir small echoes of another scene. I waited through the build-up for Mary's entrance, knowing that the Queen spoke first off-stage, that her voice came to us before she did.

It was Sarah's voice I heard. And it was Sarah who came on the stage, dressed in the elaborate fancy of that Irish talent, moving with grace and ease, laughing. The audience looked at her and were pleased by beauty for a little. But they didn't see a Queen.

That began to be pointed up. Bothwell was Bothwell, red-haired, stocky, Scots as his voice, a solid, firm, male presence, the Earl who had no pretty manners. You watched Bothwell, with Sarah a shadow in a glittering dress beside him, saying her lines neatly, like a talented amateur in a good suburban performance.

By the end of the scene I wasn't looking at the stage, because I knew what came next; I knew that in Edna's Elizabeth we'd see the Queen all right. I could hear the thumping of my heart.

'I think I'll put on my coat,' my mother whispered. 'They ought to shut those side doors, Ned.'

'Yes, Mama.'

I helped her into her coat.

'I hope it doesn't go on like this,' she said.

I knew what Angus meant about the key. The play was

181

there all right; it had the guts and the words, and the music of words, waiting for one actress to turn that key. And everything hung for that.

Edna as Elizabeth had her scene with Burghley, power with a young-old face. Her head shimmered with the jewels she was wearing on it, and every line that was given her she took and used and held sometimes. A short scene, but Mother forgot about the draught from the door, or maybe her coat kept her warm. At any rate she was quiet.

I was quiet, too. I wanted to escape from what had to come. I knew that somewhere behind those sets Sarah was waiting again for another entrance, for more minutes to be got through out on the stage in a hard light.

My feeling was remote from any sharing in imagination what Sarah was enduring. I couldn't endure with her something that was no part of me. Instead I was hollow with the love that came back from those times . . . not many . . . when we had shut away intrusions and between us held a world. I could remember that sense of experience illumined which, however false it may prove, isn't forgotten.

Sarah came on again, and this time you could see how hard Bothwell was working to shake her into some kind of life. He made a rough, hard poetry of his words, and to this Sarah returned only a kind of agonized politeness. That scene seemed to go on for ever and there was coughing in the audience. Mama whispered to me that it was hard on actors to have all that cigarette smoke about.

The curtain fell on Mary with Darnley, and the lights coming on was a kind of relief. You could hear gossip picking up just about where it had left off, and a lot of the men got up, making for exits and the nearest pub, the way they do over here at intervals when there is no bar in the theatre.

Mama began to talk to Louise and I could sit in a little hole of silence dug down through voices. I began to tell myself that after tonight Sarah must know; there wasn't room any more for the hopeful doubt and miracles. Almost everyone else on that stage had something she didn't, and they would all be hating her back there, trying to control that hatred but under this tension not able to keep it from showing. She'd be alone.

This could be where I came in. There was no need for her to face this kind of loneliness ever again, and with me there was the offer of complete escape, not even echoes following where we would go. I kept hugging that, telling myself it was what I wanted, pushing the idea down over the immediate recollection of Sarah moving through words and action with that terrible flat competence.

I don't think I would have stayed if I'd been on my own, I'd have gone and lied about that afterwards. But I couldn't produce any excuse for Mama, I couldn't even face the effort of trying. Instead I talked until I got my mother going about Dallas as the hub of the new American way, and once she was safely started on that the danger of her looking carefully into my face was averted. Or so I thought.

'Are you listening to me, Junior?'

'Sure, Mama.'

'Well, I was saying you ought to come home and see for yourself.'

'I mean to do that before I go East.'

'You mean in a few months?'

'Yes.'

'But Junior, why didn't you tell me? You've never given me the slightest hint you were coming back soon to the States.'

'Well . . . I've just thought I would. Maybe as you say I don't come home often enough.'

She was silent a moment and then she said, quite softly so no one else would hear:

'Son, you're upset. She isn't very good, is she?'

'Mama . . . please!'

'Junior! You don't need to sound bitter. You don't think I want you to be hurt?'

'No, of course not.'

'Don't try to push me away. I can see that tonight meant a lot to you. You were counting on this for her, weren't you?'

'I don't know!'

'I'm sorry,' my mother said. 'I really mean that.'

I looked at her and she did. It was a kind of break-through; it didn't mean any change in the basics between us, it didn't mean she would ever like Sarah. But she was sorry. When she put her hand on my arm and pressed it there, I was glad she had done that.

'Maybe she'll be better in the second act,' Mama said, and spoiled it all.

The second act started with a bell ringing and people pushing into seats again, feeling better from a double whisky. The lights seemed reluctant to dim and that shrilling of the bell went on and on. We scarcely had any darkness at all before the curtain thrust up and there was Rizzio singing a song to Mary and her four maids-in-waiting.

It was a scene with a quiet start, and I didn't look at Sarah at all until her voice made me, her voice clear and calm, carrying over the hall, but still the voice of a woman speaking quietly in her own private rooms.

She was sitting in a chair with a high back, wearing a dress of green with heavy embroidery, her long slim hands hanging over the ends of the chair arms. She looked completely relaxed, her quietness controlled. She was the focal point of the scene, the gently increasing tension of it emanating from her.

And then Knox came in, John Knox in caricature, the religious mountebank the author wanted him, almost grotesque. The words between Mary and the defender of Protestant Scotland caught fire and flamed. Once, in talking to him, she half-rose from her chair, the movement imperious, regal, and then checked. She sat back again, pale, her breath coming fast. The eyes of her maids were on her, and the bearded bigot. She was the centre of the pattern, giving it life. The key had turned.

There was no faltering. I lost almost all sense of Sarah there on the stage, of the girl who had said over and over these words to me on a beach. She was the Queen all right, a Queen with the power slipping from her hands, feeling the alien country all about her, these people that she would never learn to know.

She had her scene with Bothwell, the defeat of love, her voice crying out to us.

> 'God help me and all women
> Here in this world, and all men. Fair fall all chances
> The heart can long for . . . and let all women and men
> Drink deep while they can their happiness, It goes fast
> And never comes again. Mine goes with you.
> Youth, and the fund of dreams, and to lie a while
> Trusted, in arms you trust. We're alone, alone,
> Alone . . . even while we lie there we're alone,
> For it's false. It will end. Each one dies alone.'

I'd never been backstage in that theatre, never taken up Angus's invitation to come and watch rehearsals. But I found my way all right, pushing open doors and going down passages and finally coming to noise that was partly from the auditorium where they were still clapping.

But the curtain had gone down for the last time. I saw Edna standing out there and Angus with her, and others about, but no Sarah. The footlights still glared up and Edna's face looked ravaged under greasepaint, as though in that last scene between the two Queens she'd had to fight every inch of the way. She was still breathing quickly, holding Angus's hand, just standing there doing that.

'You were magnificent,' I said.

Edna nodded, as though she took that as her due, but was still caught by a sense of surprise and almost shock. Angus swung around.

'Ned. My God! You said it could happen. Did you see her . . . did you see these two?'

'Yes. Where's Sarah?'

Somebody else said it, one of the maids-in-waiting. They sent her name after her around behind the stacked sets. But I had to go off the stage, down a passage to the dressing-rooms, knocking on a door.

There was no answer. I turned the handle.

Sarah was standing facing a mirror lit by three bulbs, wearing the dully gleaming dress of the last scene, her arms at her sides. She seemed to be standing there looking at Mary. She didn't see me in the mirror at all.

'Sarah!'

She turned.

I went over and kissed her. Her cheek was ice cold.

'Hello, darling,' Sarah said, like someone who has just come back from a trip. 'Hello, darling.'

Seventeen

THE Edinburgh Festival Club is in a building used during the rest of the year for balls and occasional concerts, near Adam in styling, heavy and gloomy. The ballroom is a waste of mirrors, chandeliers and polished flooring, into which are inserted wicker chairs, and waitresses offering tea and cakes. The place is packed out by members getting their money's worth, even although it is the most uncomfortable place to eat or drink in the city. Nor are you offered the compensation of proximity to relaxing celebrities, for the big names never seem to appear, only swimming shoals of lesser fry.

It was Mama who organized an after-theatre supper party in this setting. I think she did it on an impulse resulting directly from that last scene between the two Queens, during which Mama had wept. The evening couldn't be allowed to end just there, and we were rounded up, waiting in the theatre court-yard by cars, while major members of the cast of *Mary of Scotland* came trickling out, Angus first, then the red-haired Bothwell, a couple of maids-in-waiting, Edna, and finally Sarah. Everyone was exhausted, wanting food and drink before talk could come again, but at the club we weren't able to get near the downstairs dining-room, or the upstairs cold buffet. We had to go and sit under those chandeliers while middle-aged women with sore feet carried pots of tea in and out and round about us.

I felt as though I'd been acting myself, limp. No one was looking in the least glamorous, and Bothwell had traces of his make-up still visible in his ears. Edna sat with her eyes closed a lot of the time, her face bleached-looking, chain-smoking. Sarah smoked too, and stared at a plastic table top.

These were the bleak doldrums of anticlimax and that vast room, which sent mirrored echoes of itself away into unthinkable distances, held us in a glittering emptiness. The night's effort was diminished, put in cruel perspective by the rattle of cups, and polite suburban laughter, and those inevitable plates of *gâteaux* with lurid icing. Bothwell, in gloomy irony, began to point out other groups of Festival Fringe players, also sitting in wicker chairs, looking as though life was scarcely to be endured, most of them drinking tea.

I had to hand it to Mama, she knew her duties as a hostess. When we finally got into the buffet after forty minutes of waiting she made a bid for the grand manner, perhaps remembering how easy it is to make money on the stock market if you use a woman's intuition.

'I always think,' she said, 'that an after-theatre supper should be lobster and . . . and champagne. And there's lobster on the menu.'

Angus stirred on a chair designed for the public mortification of Scottish sinners and smiled at her.

'I'll have York ham and lager,' he said.

We all had ham except Bothwell who insisted he wanted a hot meat-pie and finally got it. There was a lot of beer, some sherries, and at the end brandy. My mother's dogged determination finally turned it into a party and suddenly, in a rush, the talk about the play came. Angus started it. A full stomach had replenished his elation. He was sure he had a success on his hands, that people would come to see this play, and the critics would come and the London press would have plump paragraphs. He stepped cautiously at first into this region of his dream, and then a second brandy made everything possible.

'I tell you, the critics won't be along for at least a couple of nights, probably not this week. All the better. It'll be rolling by the time they see it. There's a good deal to be ironed out yet. We'll do it tomorrow. And now some toasts are in order. The first . . . to the girl who gave us Mary.'

Sarah looked up.

'Angus . . . please . . .!'

Angus lifted his glass.

'To Sarah.'

We all lifted glasses. There were a lot of bright smiles but Sarah just shook her head.

'Don't ask me to say anything. I can't.'

Everyone else seemed able to say something and that covered up Sarah's silence. Angus became almost heavily gallant to Mama and you could see that this evening was going to be embalmed in her memory as an occasion.

It was well after one when Sarah and I were finally alone, driving out towards the suburbs. I had the feeling she wouldn't say a word all the way to her house unless I made her. So I made her.

'Sarah, what happened tonight?'

'No one else asked that. I wonder if they were being polite? Or thought I still needed gentle handling.'

'You were dead in the part,' I said. 'And then you came alive. Why?'

'I prayed.'

There were no traffic lights and very little traffic and the car hummed over smooth asphalt.

'You're asking me to believe in a miracle?'

'If every direct answer to prayer is a miracle . . . yes.'

'You mean that . . . if you hadn't prayed nothing would have happened? You'd have gone on going through the motions and nothing more?'

'That's right.'

'Sarah, I'm sorry, but it seems too damn' easy for me. Do you mean you prayed at the end of that first act?'

'Yes. When I was lost.'

'Is it something you do quite often?'

'No. Only when I can't help it.'

'What do you mean . . . when you can't help it?'

'When I have to. When there isn't anything else . . . don't you see? No. You don't see. I've offended you. It's a little indecent, my kind of prayer. All right. But it's all I know.'

'Sarah, I'm not trying to prod at you.'

'Of course you are. You're exposing me to yourself. For the shallow little piece I am. Well . . . I'm not denying it. I've never produced any elaborate pretensions about myself . . . to you or anyone else. I'm not hiding what I do. And I'm not hiding my need, either.'

'For prayer?'

'Yes. When I'm desperate. No, that's not right. I wasn't desperate tonight, not for me. I wasn't in any danger. Even my ego would have survived. It's just that I had utter failure on my hands. And I couldn't deal with it alone.'

'You feel certain you got help?'

Suddenly Sarah laughed.

'Even you noticed the change, Ned. I've told you before I'm no great actress. I can't do what Edna does, switch herself on and off. Maybe some day, but not yet. I didn't want to talk about this, but now I don't mind. Not to you. What happened tonight wasn't just me, because I know what's in me. And I couldn't have done it.'

'All right. I'm not asking any more questions.'

'There's almost pity in your voice. You don't believe that anyone can be bigger than their natural potential. You think I had reserves for playing Mary tucked away somewhere. Well, I didn't. Not for what happened.'

'Sarah, you worked damn' hard.'

'That's right. I worked hard. I pounded the part into shape and the fact that I never got into it at all in that first act and in the rehearsals is just a form of stage fright. Or I need certain tensions worked up to a certain point in order to release my powers. Want me to go on finding answers?'

'In which you have no belief at all?'

'That's right, Ned.'

I was driving pretty slowly, dawdling along, able to watch

a drunk heaving about on the pavement. Sarah turned her head as we went past him.

'Rolling home from the Festival Club,' she said, and laughed.

'Sarah, Angus has a theory about you as an actress.'

'I'm sure it's plausible. Let's hear it.'

'He says you haven't built up your reserves yet. That you need to use experience pretty directly in your acting. He was hoping you'd use what had happened between us.'

'The pimp. Do you think I did?'

'No.'

'What makes you so sure?'

'There never has been anything between us like the thing between Mary and Bothwell in that play.'

I heard her catch her breath.

'Oh, Ned!'

'It's true. It couldn't have been us you were using.'

'It wasn't . . . there hasn't been anyone more than you Ned. And sometimes with you I've thought . . .'

'You thought you were near it?'

'That isn't what I was going to say!'

'It's what you meant, whatever you were going to say.'

The car crunched over the gravel of the Baillie drive.

'You'd better get right to bed,' I said. 'It's mighty late. But tell me one thing. Is it going to be all right, your part? Tomorrow night and the night after and the night after that?'

'Yes.'

'You're quite sure?'

'Yes.'

'Good night, honey.'

'Good night, Ned.'

Mama went to Islay and saw the shrine of our offshoot of the MacDonalds in the rain. She claimed to have found a smoke-blackened piece of hearth-stone and managed to chip off quite a large hunk. Under hotel lighting it looked like natural black rock to me, but I didn't say so. A relic, after all, is only important in the eye of the beholder, and there was no doubt that lump of stone was going to look fine when it was discretely spot-lit in a modern decor.

I contrived not to go on that little pilgrimage though I did all the arranging for it with an efficiency which startled Mama, and me, too. Nothing went wrong at all. The car I had ordered met the morning plane at Islay, whizzed Louise and Mama to as near as you could get to those mossy ruins, gave them thirty-five minutes to commune with whatever was there, and then brought them back to the plane again. We three had dinner together in Edinburgh that night, and Mama voted the whole thing a lovely experience.

During my mother's last three days in Scotland I devoted myself to being an ideal son. I hadn't much experience to help me, but I worked on the principle that what every mother really wants is attention and a feeling of continuing omnipotence over offspring who have grown in stature but not in wisdom. Once you accept a premise like this, and there's a time limit on your effort, it's possible to give an almost indelible impression of a boy likely to be the right kind of comfort to his parents' old age. My motives behind all this were mixed. I wanted to keep my mother happy and by so doing stave off a heart-to-heart about Sarah, but there was also a slightly less worthy desire to send her away with a memory picture of honest, hard-working Ned, which was going to make her a little less tolerant of Sam. My brother, of course, had failed his College Boards again. The news of that had reached Italy.

'We'll have to give him another chance to sit, of course,' Mama said in the ruins of the Royal Chapel at Holyrood House. 'He's just got to go to college.'

'Why?'

'Ned! You went to college.'

'Sure, and I worked summers as a waiter. Remember? There wasn't all that much money around in those days.'

'Now Ned, you know that we didn't ask you to work. That was an idea of yours.'

'It's not the sort of idea Sam's ever had?'

'It's all a question of conditioning. The psychiatrist says that Sam suffered from an emotional trauma when he was small.'

'Oh. I suppose that can be serious?'

'It can be terribly serious. You're an extrovert, you always have been. That way you're really like your father. He's . . . well . . . a businessman with simple enough motivations.'

'Are you thinking that maybe Sam gets his genes from the MacDonalds?'

Mama lifted her eyes to chunks of ruined masonry, thoughtfully.

'It could be. After all, your great-grandfather was an exile. There's a kind of heritage of insecurity there. It might even be something dormant that's come out in Sam. There's no doubt about it, he needs intelligent and attentive understanding.'

I gave up. There could be no shifting of that focus on Sam. And just then I caught Louise looking at me, a girl almost continuously silent ever since the departure of Tommy to catch his ship. Now something glimmered in her eyes that could be a spark of sympathy. Maybe she'd had to grow up, too, without anyone hunting in her for traumas.

The next morning in the station we all smiled at each other on the platform and then Mama and Louise got into their compartment and smiled through glass. There was a little hatch that could be opened, just big enough for Mama's head and she used it.

'We're not saying good-bye, Ned, we'll be seeing you so soon.'

'Sure. Practically right away.'

I was safe enough now, she couldn't possibly start on Sarah through that hatch, not when the guard might blow the whistle at any moment.

'Ned, I'm sorry we didn't manage to see Sarah and her father again. You'll say good-bye to them for us?'

'Of course, Mama.'

'I do like him. I'm sure your father would like him, too.

193

I said for him to come out and see us in Texas the next time he's in the States.'

'Well, I guess he'd see a lot of new building out there. And that's his line. Maybe he'll take you up on that.'

Mama went on smiling.

'Sarah doesn't seem terribly interested in America.'

'Oh, she likes little places. Where you can drive from one edge to the other in a day.'

'In that case she wouldn't much like Texas.'

'Well, certainly we're different there.'

'I thought her acting was just wonderful, Ned. Are you going to go and see the play again tonight?'

'I can't tonight. It's Sunday.'

'Of course. I forgot. It's been most interesting getting in with theatre people. I never knew what they were like before. I don't expect it's an experience you'll have much of when you leave Scotland.'

'Well, of course there will be the native ballet out in Sumatra.'

'You mean those girls that wear those head-dresses and can move pieces of themselves? Don't you go and fall for one of them, Ned!'

I grinned at her and Mama laughed. Then she pushed her head a little bit more through that hatch.

'I know that everything is all right with you, son. I just know it.'

'Yes, Mama.'

I didn't hear the guard's whistle but the train shivered. Louise, shut away by glass, began to wave both hands. Mama started to cry.

'Don't do that,' I said. 'I'll be home before you're settled in.'

'I know. That's what I'm counting on. Ned . . . you won't do anything silly?'

'No, Mama.'

The train was really moving now, rumbling away with a kind of British decorum. My mother put a handkerchief through the hatch and waggled it up and down. I could see Louise's hands at the window.

Beyond the platforms, in the centre area, there was a hint of sunshine coming through smoky glass. I went to the bookstall and got all the Sunday papers likely to deal with the Festival, even the ones that might squeeze in some kind of comment between cheesecake slabs of female flesh. I took them to my car and sat there reading.

Angus had made it all right. In one of the two papers which matter his production got twenty lines, and he was named, as were Sarah and Edna and Bothwell. In the other there was even more, a hint of warmth, a kind of welcome to a Scottish effort at this Festival where the drama seems to be the thing they think about last. One of the gossip papers had a feature on Angus and his new job and his new importance in the local scene which read suspiciously like a hand-out he'd written himself sitting under the portrait of youth lost. In another Edna had a picture which made her unrecognizably lush.

I got out and went over to a call-box and rang through to the Baillie home. After only two buzzes Sarah answered.

'You lout! I've been waiting for you to call. Did you sleep in or something?'

'I've just waved Mama off.'

'Oh, heavens, I forgot! Sorry.'

'It's all right. Congratulations and everything. You've got all the papers?'

'Naturally. Oh, Ned. I'm hugging myself. I'm still in bed. We've got a new early who's a jewel. She likes to bring up trays. And all these came with it.'

'Sarah, I'm as excited as if I'd something to do with it myself.'

'Sweet. You had. You've kept me from going potty. There have been times I was awfully near it. Ned . . . everyone's phoned me. I might almost be lying in my suite in the Dorchester. I know it isn't quite that, but it almost feels like it. Ned, they liked it. Even the gloomy boys from London. They weren't just patronizing, were they?'

'No. I wouldn't say they were patronizing at all. I think they felt they'd had a good night at *Mary of Scotland* and before it's over there'll be thousands who think that.'

'Oh . . . go on. I can just lap it up. When did you get the Sunday papers?'

'Just now. I gave Mama a batch to take with her, but I didn't peek. I didn't dare.'

'I hope you gave her a message from me? She was . . . she was nice to me.'

I laughed.

'Well, she was!' Sarah said loudly.

'Uh-huh. Am I going to see you today?'

'Lunch? And Ned, before I forget, keep next Saturday. Angus is throwing a party. For all the cast and attachments. You qualify with a special mention. I think he's deeply grateful to you.'

When I got back to my car there was a policeman standing by it, a young man with a solemn expression, and great dignity from the domed helmet.

'This is not a waiting area,' he said. 'You have left this vehicle here for three-quarters of an hour.'

I held out my hand.

'I'll take my ticket quietly.'

He looked at me, then the car, gloomily remembering the special courtesy for the Festival instructions.

'Are you away now, sir?'

'If you release me . . . at once.'

'Och well, away you go then.'

Angus's party had more attachments than cast. The Adam drawing-room bulged. Everyone seemed to have come on from the last performance of the second week and no one had bothered to dress up much; it wasn't that kind of party.

One wall was the bar, a row of tables covered with cloths and bottles and glasses and food. You served yourself and then joined the shouting.

I was a little surprised, rather feeling that Angus would have made a party of his strike a tone, perhaps something like claret mulled with red-hot pokers by hired youths in white jackets, but this seemed more of a gigantic bid to get rid of ten years of social obligations.

'Splendid to see you,' he bellowed in my ear. 'What are you doing these days? Why don't you come behind scenes with us? You know you can just walk in.'

'Thanks, but I'm listening to music . . . when I get up to town. But the world's still going on out in Grangemouth. Oil for the diesel cars, you know. And I have to make up some of the time I spent with my mother.'

'She was an absolute pet,' he howled, and then clutched at somebody else's arm.

I caught a glimpse of Sarah over in a corner talking to Bothwell, both of them holding glasses and shaking with laughter.

'Hello,' Edna said, from only two bodies away.

I pushed over and found her glass empty, and pushed away again. She gave me a smile when I got back.

'You don't look as happy as the rest of us, Ned.'

'I haven't got your reasons. I saw more good news in the papers this week.'

Edna laughed.

'You mean the local press? Yes, they held off for the London reaction before folding us into the Scottish bosom.'

'I saw the play again on Thursday. It seemed to me better than ever. You're holding it all right.'

'Things never looked back from that first night. But aren't you sick of it? I didn't see you on Thursday.'

'I didn't come backstage.'

'You mean . . . Sarah didn't even know you were there?'

'That's right.'

'Ned, there's something about you which stirs up the maternal in me. You're not going to be in Scotland very long now, are you?'

'No.'

'And you think you've lost all your chances.'

I looked at her.

'I guess so. You warned me once against thinking I had any.'

'I know. I shouldn't have done. I knew all about Sarah, but I was wrong.'

'Don't start liking her. It would ruin your last week.'

Edna laughed.

'There's no danger. Will you listen to me again?'

'Uh-huh.'

'Well . . . this isn't just a party. I shouldn't give you this hint, but I've got to. Milling about in this mess is every representative of the press that Angus could collect.'

'I thought the need for that was over?'

'It's only beginning. You'll find out in about twenty minutes. And that's all I can say. Angus is waiting until a certain ripeness has been achieved. I suggest you work your way over towards Sarah.'

'Edna, what are you trying to tell me?'

'It's a kind of tentative good deed. Go on!'

It took me all of that twenty minutes to get over to Sarah. On the way a girl I recognized as a walk-on in *Mary of Scotland* put her arms around my neck and kissed me. 'You're sweet,' she said. I think she thought I was someone else, maybe a dramatic critic. Or a talent spotter. At the Festival anyone can be anybody.

Sarah was still talking to Bothwell, but she saw me and put out her hand. I took it.

'We're on shop, Ned. That's when we're at our most boring. . . .'

'Ladies and gentlemen,' Angus roared. 'Your attention a moment, please!'

He was standing by the fireplace, not very far from us and both his hands were in the air, palms towards us. The roar abated and the sudden silence was almost astonishing. A girl coughed and couldn't stop. Angus waited.

'I have an announcement,' he said. 'And I think this is the appropriate moment. Three days ago I was approached by a man whose name will be known to every one of you connected with the theatre and most of you who are not. These meetings were in confidence, and I have only been empowered this evening to give you my news. I can say that it is pretty startling news. And the man concerned is none other than the great London impresario, Sir Mitcham Reed.'

Angus paused. Everyone stared at him. Sarah's hand tightened against mine.

'Sir Mitcham has gone back to London. He proposes to put on *Mary of Scotland* for a limited season down there.'

There was a roar then. Angus waved his hands.

'Wait! Wait! There's more to come. Sir Mitcham says he has hopes of getting a theatre within two months. He proposes to take the entire production as it stands south. . . .'

The roar swelled up again, drowning Angus's shouts.

'Wait! Wait! I'm not finished. I've told Sir Mitcham that my Scottish commitments make it impossible for me to go south as the London producer of *Mary of Scotland*. He told me that he didn't really think that mattered any more, that the play now has its shape and he has every confidence that all of you will be able to hold that shape in the West End. He is, however, going to appoint another producer for London, as it is right he should do. I needn't tell you how sorry I am not to be coming. But I now feel that my opportunity . . . my real opportunity . . . is here in Scotland.'

'Ned,' Sarah said softly beside me. 'Oh, Ned!'

I went on holding her hand. I was waiting for something more. It came.

'Ladies and gentlemen, this is a time for rejoicing, there's no doubt about that. But I'm deeply sorry to have to say that there is one feature of all this which saddens me. I said the entire production as it now stands . . . but unfortunately that wasn't quite accurate. As you will all understand Sir Mitcham, in spite of his position, has to minimize his risks in a profession as hazardous as this. He told me that personally he wouldn't have changed any detail of the production. But he has his backers to consider. And conditions these days dictate policy.

To ensure the success of the play he felt that he must give the title role to a West End actress.'

There was no roar then, just a dead silence. Sarah in her corner was hidden by me, and I went on hiding her. Above us Angus's voice boomed.

'There is no need for me to tell you how Sarah Baillie has played Mary of Scotland. We've seen that for ourselves, night after night. Sir Mitcham himself told me how moved he had been by her performance. He doesn't like what he has to do any more than we like to see it done. But it is one of those things which happen in our profession and we just have to take.'

I had to look at Sarah then. She was standing quite still, erect, so pale that her make-up made her face the mask it could be when she used too much. Then her lips moved and I saw her tongue touch the upper one.

Behind us was a stirring in the packed mob. Angus shouted out again:

'Gentlemen. There's a phone in my bedroom. And a box just down the street.'

The press were leaving us.

'Sarah.'

'Hello, Ned.'

She smiled.

'To hell with them,' Bothwell said. 'I won't go either.'

She swung on him.

'Don't be a fool! Take your chance.'

Angus was beside us.

'Sarah,' he said. 'I know that was clumsy. I've been thinking all night how to do it.'

Sarah's voice was even, low.

'You did it very well, Angus. Who is the West End actress?'

'It's not fixed, but Sir Mitcham hopes to get Beryl Verne.'

'I thought she was in Hollywood?'

'She's expected back next week, Sarah.'

'Beryl Verne,' Bothwell spat it out. 'She used to be blonde, didn't she? With a splendid photogenic emphasis on the lung warts. Mary of Scotland! I'm going to pour myself the biggest drink I have ever poured.'

Angus went away, following Bothwell. Sarah said softly:

'Do you mind just standing there a minute, Ned? I'm not quite ready for them yet. And I'll take my drink. It's over there.'

'Finish it,' I said, giving it to her.

'Good idea.'

Her face was still dead white.

'How do I look?'

'Take a couple of very deep breaths, Sarah.'

'Hm. Yes, that is better, even with the smoke. What is it, an old Texas trick?'

Edna came up behind us.

'Sarah, I know you don't want people saying this. But I must. I've been feeling horrible.'

'Been? How long have you known?'

'Well . . . Angus had to tell someone.'

'Of course. Don't let it worry you, darling. If they had to cut someone out I was probably the best choice. I need a lot of experience yet. Think of the panic I caused at the start. How are you looking forward to playing with Beryl Verne? Have you seen her act?'

'Yes. She's not just a film star. She's pretty good and will be much better.'

Sarah smiled.

'Darling, I knew I could stretch your generosity to the breaking point. You ought to have said you were dreading it.'

'Sarah, I didn't mean . . .'

'Of course not! You know, Edna, I think I might take over from you. I have the feeling in my bones that when this play comes off you'll have other offers down in London.'

Edna smiled.

'Character parts,' Sarah added.

Edna's smile stayed, held there.

'Scotland is going to need a new queen on the spot,' Sarah said. 'I think I'll start grooming myself.'

Angus came back with drinks and Sarah caught his arm.

'Angus, will you groom me for a great future under your star?'

'I was hoping you'd see it that way, Sarah.'

'Of course I see it that way. You handled things well tonight. To wait until the party was solid. And gin's such a good anæsthetic.'

'Sarah, you're not to mind!'

She looked at him, smiling.

'I'm jealous, I think. I don't want anyone else to do Mary in that play. I feel as if . . . Oh, I'm a fool. Do you mind if Ned and I go away now? Everyone is hoping we will.'

The Baillie house was empty when we got back to it. Eileen was staying with friends in England and James Baillie, back home again, was making his first tentative sortie as a widower into his Edinburgh social world, a civic reception for a German symphony orchestra. He told his daughter that he might be meeting friends afterwards and be rather late.

We went into the beige living-room, Sarah walking a little in front of me trailing a fur stole from one hand. She dropped it on the carpet and turned almost slowly to me.

'They didn't really mind. Not one of them. I hate them. . . .'

I caught her and held her.

'Oh, Ned!'

'Darling, don't!'

'Let me wail! I've wanted to. All the way home.'

'Okay, you wail.'

I picked her up and took her to the sofa and sat on it holding her. She had her head against my shoulder, her face hidden. When she was quiet I said:

'Sarah, all that about following Angus's star . . .?'

'No!'

'You didn't mean it?'

'No! I want to go away, Ned. With you. Will you take me?'

'Will I take you! Don't be silly!'

'Palembang,' she said. 'Remember how we talked about that? It isn't very big, is it?'

'No, not very big, Sarah.'

'I'll like that. What will your mother say, Ned?'

She leaned back then and looked at me; the tears had made her mascara run and smudge her cheeks.

'Mama will say that you're not the girl she'd have chosen for me. But then no girl a man really wants ever is.'

'I'll be very dutiful, Ned. What about your father?'

'You'll like him.'

'You mean . . . I really will like him?'

'Yes.'

'What an odd thought. But comforting. Like you. Without you I don't know . . . Ned, it isn't true, is it? What Mary says about love? "For it's false. It will end." '

'No, it's not true, honey. She was unlucky.'

'Yes. Poor Mary. And the Ednas go glittering on. I'm tired, Ned.'

'I'll take you up to bed.'

I carried her up those carpeted stairs that gave no sound. Her room was like the other rooms in this house, carefully prepared for human occupation and immune to it. The furniture was walnut, the single bed had a quilted and buttoned satin headboard. There were soft lights and firm lights where needed and a couple of door switches put them all on.

Sarah had dressed here to go to the theatre and for the party afterwards, but there was nothing lying around; the pots of face cream reflected by mirrors might have been put there by the courtesy of the makers.

'Let me down,' she said. 'You can't stay up here. Daddy will be back.'

'I wasn't thinking of staying. Where are your things?'

She looked at me.

'I'm to be put to bed? No one's done that this way for a long time. But you're right, I rather need it. You'll find my nightie behind that long mirror. You'll find it on a hook. Remember, I use wool even in the summer?'

'I remember.'

She began to undress, folding her things as she did it, but I took them from her and held out the brushed wool nightie.

She put up her arms and slipped into it. Then she went over to the wash-basin and, without looking in the mirror, began to scrub her teeth like a child would do it, a kind of frenzied vigour before collapsing into tiredness, her arm jiggling.

Sarah came padding back across thick carpeting in bare feet.

'What about your make-up?' I said.

'Oh, heavens!'

'It's all right, get into bed. I'll bring you a face-cloth.'

She sat propped up against pillows, waiting for the cloth, and took it from me almost solemnly, doing her duty, rubbing her cheeks and into her eyes and up to her hair.

'Better, Ned?'

'Much.'

When I was at the basin again Sarah said suddenly:

'Is a lot of marriage like this? Bringing face-cloths to your dearie when she needs them?'

'I guess so.'

'I'm going to like that. Ned, what will you say to Papa if you meet him in the front hall?'

'I won't meet him. I'm going now. I'll be back tomorrow afternoon, latish.'

She held out her arms to me. I knelt by the bed and she held on to me hard.

'You . . . Oh, Ned.'

In a minute I said:

'Honey, are you all right?'

'Yes. Now.'

'And you're going to sleep?'

'Yes, Ned. You'll put out the lights?'

'I'll put out the lights as I go,' I said.

Eighteen

I HAD to work that Sunday morning and most of the afternoon, too. When I left Grangemouth it was after five and by the time I got into the city a sky thickly wadded by cloud was bringing an early night. The gas lamps were already lit all along the high-walled back roads and the air had a bite in it that could almost be frost. It was September.

I took the wide sweep for the Baillie gates and then had to brake. A taxi was coming down towards me. It pulled into the side and I moved on again.

British taxis tend to hide their passengers, but I saw who was in this one. Angus.

At the top of the gravelled rise I yanked on the hand-brake and jumped out, but the taxi was gone, in a little burst of speed. I could hear it droning away.

The door was opened by one of the dailies, a middle-aged woman who looked as though she might have been just ready to put on her hat.

'Miss Baillie?'

'She's in the drawing-room.'

I didn't wait for any announcements. Sarah was standing by the fire, alone in there. I closed the door behind me. It was a long way from me to her, but I could feel something in that room and see it from the way she looked at me.

'I saw Angus. How long has he been here?'

She didn't make any movement towards me.

'About an hour, I suppose.'

'What was he offering, Sarah?'

'Oh . . . a lot of things.'

I went towards her. My voice was loud.

'You listened?'

'Ned, don't shout at me!'

'I've got a right, haven't I? Everything was fixed last night, wasn't it?'

Sarah put out a hand and touched the tiles behind her. It was trembling a little, the long fingers feeling for something to hold and not finding it.

'Ned, last night I slept for a bit. And then I woke up and you were gone. And it wasn't real.'

'I had to go, you know that!'

'Yes, I know it. Ned, don't bully me, please!'

'What is it, Sarah? What has that man said to you?'

'It isn't what he said. It's what I know!'

'Well?'

'I can't. I can't go with you. I can't go where you go.'

I stood very still. And the thing which had been waiting for me, which I had felt the moment I stood in that room, moved into my heart. Sarah wasn't even looking at me; she was staring down at the hearth-rug that was a Persian which could have been made in a factory.

'If you don't come with me, what will you do?'

'I . . . I'm going to Glasgow.'

'To be under Angus's star?'

'That's only part. A small part. It's the chance I have been offered now. But I . . . if Angus hadn't come today I still would have known.'

'I don't believe it.'

'It's true. Oh, Ned. I want everything you can give me, but I haven't enough to give back.'

'That's for me to say.'

'No. It might be now. It wouldn't be later. Don't you see? I don't claim to be a good actress. I may never learn to be one.

But I've got to go on trying. There is no other way for me, that's all.'

'As my wife you'd be wasted, is that it?'

'Oh, please . . . don't twist things. But I can't find a compromise this way, Ned. Going with you wouldn't give me my chance to do what I have to do. What we had together . . . well . . . it would be proved false.'

'I don't believe it!'

'I know. I know what I am. I can't give you what you want. I never have. Ned, I never gave you enough, even when I wanted to, so much. It's me, do you hear? It's nothing to do with you. Nothing at all.'

'Sarah! For God's sake come out of this. It's Angus's talk. Do you want to become like Edna? The little queen? A patched-up life?'

She looked at me then.

'You can call it that, I suppose. But Edna has had other chances, to make a different kind of life. She was married once. It didn't work. But they can't divorce, and that's that. She has to go on with the knowledge that she's failed. And I think she believes it's a sin to have allowed something to become more important to her than her marriage. They do feel that way.'

'What's all this to you? You're no Catholic. You could even say you're free to experiment. I'm only asking you to give me a chance.'

'And I can see the end if I did that.'

'Oh, God! Sarah! If I go out of this room now, I'm not coming back. You know that. If you send me away now, that's it!'

She stood looking down at the carpet. I knew perfectly well that if I went over and took her in my arms I could break through what was happening. She wanted to be in my arms. But it would be a postponement. The thing that had been waiting for me in this room would be waiting again another day. I began to talk.

'What are you afraid of? The big world outside your

village? There are other villages, all over the place. Plenty of them. I'm going to settle, I told you that. I'm not going to wander all my days. I'm only doing it now because . . . well, it's a phase in my business, that's all. I get sent here and there, yes. But it won't go on, Sarah. Does your village have to be Scotland?'

She didn't answer.

'I'd even live here if you wanted, Sarah. I . . . I like Scotland. I've grown used to it. There's a good life here if you make it. Maybe that wasn't just a joke about going into your father's business. I'm not in love with what I do, or the life it gives me. Why shouldn't I go in for putting up buildings? I could probably get damn' interested. After all, it's a kind of service, isn't it?'

'Stop this, Ned!'

'I tell you I'm ready to give up things on my side!'

'No! I can't take you from your life. You can't take me from mine. That's all there is to it.'

I knew she was right, there was no answer. Angus coming here today with his promises had only pushed her quickly towards the thing she had to see. And I had to see, too. My body was shivering, but the shouting was gone from my heart and from my mind.

'Sarah, what's left? To say we'll remember a green island?'

She put her hands over her face.

'Oh . . . please go.'

I went. It was really beginning to get dark when I got outside, September dark, winter coming again. I had to watch the steps going down them; going down them away from that house that didn't offer any light behind you. I got into the car and sat behind the wheel. I began to cry. I couldn't stop it, not for a minute or two, not until I got out my handkerchief and wiped it all over my face, not only my eyes.

Then I started the car, switching on the lights, driving off. In half a minute I was out in the road leading to Morningside station, a road lined with dark trees and that grey stone. I reached-out and switched on the radio.

It was the American Forces Network in Germany, dance music. I was back in my own world, travelling in it, quite alone, cut off from that other. I was where I had to be, taking the road to Grangemouth from the city. And then the road from there.